'You're makin … **said, quite un** … **was clearly noting her flushed face.**

'Good,' he said, grinning at her.

It's pathetic, really, she chided herself. The first good-looking, charming man you come into contact with, you turn into a quivering jelly because you've been deprived for so long.

She wondered if he could divine something of her reaction to him, hoping fervently that it was not the case. After all, she knew nothing about him…

Rebecca Lang trained to be a State Registered Nurse in Kent, England, where she was born. Her main focus of interest became operating theatre work, and she gained extensive experience in all types of surgery on both sides of the Atlantic. Now living in Toronto, Canada, she is married to a Canadian pathologist and has three children. When not writing, Rebecca enjoys gardening, reading, theatre, exploring new places, and anything to do with the study of people.

Recent titles by the same author:

THE SURGEON'S CONVENIENT FIANCÉE
NURSE ON ASSIGNMENT

A FATHER
FOR HER SON

BY
REBECCA LANG

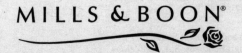
MILLS & BOON®

All the characters in this book have no existence outside the imagination of the author, and have no relation whatsoever to anyone bearing the same name or names. They are not even distantly inspired by any individual known or unknown to the author, and all the incidents are pure invention.

First published in Great Britain 2007
Harlequin Mills & Boon Limited,
Eton House, 18-24 Paradise Road, Richmond, Surrey TW9 1SR

© Rebecca Lang 2007

ISBN-13: 978 0 263 85252 3

Set in Times Roman 10½ on 12¾ pt
03-0707-50747

Printed and bound in Spain
by Litografia Rosés, S.A., Barcelona

A FATHER
FOR HER SON

CHAPTER ONE

SHE had never seen the inside of a private detective's office before. Now she looked around her, trying not to stare too obviously in front of the secretary who had a desk in the corner of the small waiting room.

In films and novels such offices were rather barren and somewhat seedy. This one was a little better than that, a cut above, although it gave the impression that the owners were trying to keep a low profile.

The secretary stood up. 'Come in, Ms Grey. Mr Smythe will see you now.'

'Thank you.' They went along a narrow passage, bordered on both sides by small rooms. They were in an old house, on the second floor, where everything was suitably anonymous, including the clients and, she assumed, the detectives.

'Wait in here, Ms Grey. He'll be along in a few minutes. Have a seat.'

The room was similarly nondescript, with a large desk, filing cabinets, three reasonably comfortable chairs.

Anna Grey subsided gratefully into the most comfortable-looking chair on the door side of the desk, forcing herself to try to relax and not question too much her decision to come here. Certainly over the past few weeks she had been indecisive, then had finally made up her mind.

Even so, there was a certain dissonance in her mind, as well as nervousness. As she waited, she mused about her reasons for being there, as she had done for a long time prior to that moment.

There was a last time for everything, she thought, although frequently we didn't know it was the last time; if we did, perhaps we would pay more attention to the events preceding it.

She would never forget the night when everything had changed, when Simon had seemingly disappeared off the face of the earth. For her, that had been the night of the beginning of a loss of innocence, the start of that period of her life when she had understood what it meant to really grow up. It had started when she had waited for Simon and he had not arrived; he had never arrived after that.

'Ms Grey?' The detective came into the room, quickly and silently. 'Please, don't get up.' He extended a hand. 'I'm Hector Smythe.'

He was short and thin, totally bald, the skin of his scalp shiny, and his face was wizened, making Anna think of an elf.

'Thank you for seeing me,' she said hastily, shaking his hand. 'I'm still not sure I should be here, taking up your time. This is the last resort, you understand?'

'Yes, I do understand. Please, don't apologise. Most people say something similar when they come to see us here,' he said as he seated himself at the big desk and fixed her with a shrewd, intelligent stare from alert brown eyes. 'Your problem is obviously severe enough for you to want to seek help. That's good enough for us. That's what we're here for, and we're certainly not going to waste your money. If we can't help you, we say so right from the outset. Believe me, all problems are equally fascinating, otherwise we wouldn't be in the business. Now…let me see…'

Instead of the usual computer, he opened a simple manila folder that was already on the desk, and Anna found herself admiring the economy and simplicity of the place.

'Don't trust computers,' he said, apparently reading her mind. 'They are not secure. Neither are cellphones.'

Anna nodded, smiling, relieved that her personal information would be totally safe with him.

'There's nothing that can't be retrieved by an expert from a computer,' he went on, warming to his theme. 'Of course, we do use computers for some things, for searches, for instance, but we put nothing personal on them, either about ourselves or anyone else. We have here a man who does forensic data retrieval for us. He's a genius, in my opinion. Otherwise, in this business, often old-fashioned methods are best. Speak to people face to face when you can.'

Anna nodded again, impressed and already feeling more at ease. A week before coming to this interview she had given details of her case history to the secretary over the telephone—a land line that the woman had assured her, unasked, was not tapped. The agency specialised in tracing missing persons, counter-industrial espionage and surveillance in marital infidelity.

'I have some news for you,' Hector Smythe said, looking up, smiling. 'We have located a Dr S.A. Ruelle right here in the city, right here in Gresham, Ontario.' He beamed across the desk at her.

'Oh!' Anna's cheeks flushed with a sudden rush of blood as her heart leapt in anticipation and renewed hope. 'Oh.'

'Mind you,' he went on, 'the two first names are not the same as the ones you gave me, but those can be changed. He calls himself Seth Alexi Ruelle. It seems more than coincidence that the initials should be the same. The surname is unusual enough that there can't be too many doctors with that name and the right initials.'

'No.' She stared at him, scarcely able to breathe, even more nervous now as all sorts of questions rushed through her mind. If Simon were here in Gresham, why wouldn't he have contacted her or returned to his job at the hospital? After all, she was easy enough to find, even though she had left her job at Gresham General Hospital recently to look after her son. Her hopes had suddenly skyrocketed and then plunged again as she'd looked at the problem from a common sense point of view.

'We are in the process of checking where he trained,' Hector Smythe went on. 'We've managed to access the Medical Association files for the province, which are available to the public, if you know where to look, to ascertain that he is registered as a medical practitioner in Ontario. As you know, a doctor cannot practise here without being registered.'

'Yes.'

'According to the records, he trained in Boston. But I think the graduation dates may not be quite right for your Dr Simon Ruelle, so that makes me doubt that he's Simon, but we're going to check him out anyway. This doctor seems somewhat older than your man would have been, I think. Do you know when Simon graduated?' He looked at her across the expanse of the large desk.

Again, Anna flushed. 'I don't actually know,' she admitted, shamefacedly. 'There are certain things I don't know about him, that perhaps I should know, but, you see, I sort of accepted him at face value and didn't ask an awful lot of questions in the time that we knew each other.'

'Not very wise,' he said softly, looking sad.

'You see…it all seemed so…right…our being together.'

'It usually does, at least for a time,' he said gently, looking at her kindly and seriously, with only a hint of cynicism in his demeanour.

'Let me just get you to confirm a few things that my secretary wrote here, Ms Grey,' Hector Smythe continued, breaking into her jumbled thoughts. 'You have a three-year-old son, fathered by a Dr Simon Angelo Ruelle."

'I… Yes,' she said. 'Yes, I have a son.'

'Forgive me for asking this, but I must yet again, Ms Grey, although I know my secretary asked it. Is it at all possible that this Dr Simon Ruelle knew of your pregnancy and did a moonlight flit?'

Anna smiled wanly. 'No, he didn't know,' she said emphatically. 'At that point, I hadn't told anybody. I was going to tell him on the day he disappeared. I know that seems significant, but it couldn't have been.'

'Mmm. It does seem a little too convenient for him that he should have disappeared just at the time you needed him. Not that I wish to say or imply that he would not have wanted to be with you, or support you. It is merely something that we must consider, seeing as it is a very common mode of behaviour, as you must know.'

'Oh, yes. But he didn't come back to his job. He had been accepted into a surgical residency training programme, which is not easy to get into. There was no way that he would have given that up unless something serious had happened to him. I was not able to make enquiries on my own because I was not next of kin. No one would talk to me because of issues of privacy. We were not even engaged or living together. I had only known him really well for four months. That was the time we were going out together…' Her voice trailed away, a familiar feeling of hopelessness coming over her.

'Let me see what we have here…' Hector Smythe said, consulting the brief notes in front of him. 'Simon Ruelle was born in Zimbabwe, trained in Boston, came to Gresham, Ontario to take up a surgical fellowship at Gresham General Hospital here while he was waiting for the surgical residency training to begin. Is that right?'

'Yes. That was going on for four years ago,' she said. 'I met him in the operating suite of that hospital, where I was working as a nurse. I've recently given up my job to look after my son and to help my mother take care of my father temporarily…he's been ill, and needed an operation.'

'Is he going to be all right?'

'Yes, I'm pretty sure he will be. He had prostate cancer, which was in the early stages, thank God. It hasn't spread so the prognosis is good. Before that happened, my mother was looking after Finn, my son, while I worked part time,' she explained, feeling more at ease talking about her everyday life.

'I see. It certainly seems very odd that this Dr Ruelle should have disappeared just then.'

'His fellowship would have soon ended,' she confirmed, 'and he was so much looking forward to starting the residency. He felt privileged to be there. I think something awful must have happened to him.'

'Is it possible, do you think, that the offer of the residency

could have been withdrawn from him at the last moment?'
Hector Smythe said.

'I…don't think so. That's something that hadn't occurred
to me.' She stammered slightly. 'I—I think he would have told
me, and he would have been upset, to say the least. When I
last saw him, when I worked with him, he seemed on top of
the world. Even when he knew his mother was not well, he
didn't think it was anything serious.'

The man opposite her looked at her steadily. Although his
face was bland, his expression nonjudgmental, she knew he
must be thinking she was naïve. Well, she was, and she knew
it. At least, she had been. Being a mother, especially without
a significant other, made one grow up fast.

'Don't you worry, we'll find him,' Hector Smythe said. 'If
this Dr Ruelle is not the right one, it's possible, perhaps, he
may be able and willing to help us to locate him, as he has
inside information about the workings of the medical profession. The profession is a small one in the sense that medical
information is shared the world over—there are international
meetings, co-operation in research and all those things which
will work in our favour. So, what I want you to do, Ms Grey,
is go round there where he has his office and take a look at
him.'

He made it sound so easy, like going to look at a house
that was for sale or something, while she was consumed with
feelings of apprehension.

For another twenty minutes they continued to talk, then
Hector Smythe stood up. 'If you are in agreement, Ms Grey,
you can see Dr Seth Ruelle today. If he is not the right one,
you may as well see him to rule him out right away. That will
save us a lot of legwork and undercover stuff.'

Anna stood up too, not particularly flattered by the broad hint that if this man was Simon he might be scared away from her. 'I can see him today?' she said incredulously, with that nervous, sick excitement that one felt in anticipation of a longed-for moment.

'We took the liberty of making an appointment for you, by saying that we were looking for a missing person and that he might be able to help us,' he said. 'I doubt that he is Simon Ruelle, as Simon would most likely not return to Gresham to practise medicine, having left it so abruptly. I have to say that your name appeared not to mean anything to him but, then, we did not tell him the whole story. You will have to explain yourself more fully when you get there. Considering that we were not willing to give him much information over the telephone, he was very gracious in agreeing to help us. I thought it better if you explained the situation to him, face to face.'

'It does seem a bit…er…cloak and dagger,' she said, smiling.

'Yes, it does.' He laughed. 'That's how we prefer to operate. And I told him so.'

Anna decided not to ask any more questions just then. She would just go with the flow for now. 'All right. Thank you,' she said. 'I'm very grateful.' Events were moving on faster than she had anticipated after years of stalemate and frustration.

'How old are you, Ms Grey?' he said. 'I don't seem to have that information here. And I'd like your son's exact age. I'd also like some other information, about your professional training, and so on…just in case at some time in the future you need to claim financial support.'

Anna subsided into the chair again. 'I'm twenty-seven,' she said. 'I started my nursing training at the university here in Gresham when I was eighteen. And I graduated four years later.'

'I see. And your work experience?'

'When I was at university I worked for a good part of each summer at Gresham General Hospital, then, after graduation, I got a permanent job there. I went to work in the operating suite in October of that year—that's when I met Simon. We…we became seriously involved the next year.'

'You were twenty-two when you met him?'

'Yes.'

'And what about Finn?'

'He was born on the first of April, three years ago,' she said. 'He was actually due to be born on the twenty-second of March, but first babies are often late.'

It had not taken her long to realise she had fallen pregnant, but it had taken her longer to summon up courage to tell Simon. She had left it too late.

'How old is Simon?' he asked.

'He's…um…thirty-one now,' she calculated.

'It's almost certain that this Dr Seth Ruelle is not Simon, as from some preliminary enquiries we've been able to make, he's a few years older. However, not to worry. We really want to elicit his help. Now, our secretary, Janet, will give you the instructions about where he is.' He flicked back his sleeve to look at his watch. 'It's in the old medical arts building on the edge of the university campus. You have three-quarters of an hour in which to get there.'

'I know the place. Thank you.'

'Don't get your hopes up too much right now,' he said

kindly. 'This is just a start and it may get us somewhere eventually by association, with the names being the same. Could you call me later today to let me know what happened?'

'Yes. Goodbye,'

On the ground floor of the house she went into the women's washroom and stared at her pale face in a mirror, knowing that she looked tired and washed out, certainly not ready to meet someone who might be able to help her. Being a mother of a young child and helping her parents in a time of crisis were taking their toll on her. Often she felt that her first flush of youthful beauty had gone. With her very pale skin, her fine, straight fair hair and blue eyes, which had a haunted quality, she looked like a waif. Hastily she added a touch of lipstick to her very pale lips.

Having answered Mr Smythe's questions, she now relived some of the anxiety she had felt when getting up her courage to break the news to Simon, then the despair she had experienced when he had disappeared.

Out in the street she put up her umbrella against the cold autumn rain, glad of the little partially closed-off world that it enabled her to inhabit as she hurried along the wet pavement towards the nearest bus station. She needed time to think, when there was little time. Still not sure whether she was doing the right thing in pursuing Simon, it seemed that events were carrying her along, not entirely within her control. Well, she had started the ball rolling again and to a certain extent she must have the courage to follow where it took her. It was required of her to go with the flow.

If the Dr Ruelle she was about to see was indeed Simon, what would he think of her now? Presumably he had agreed to see her of his own free will. He could have refused. Now that she was out of the detective's office, she could think of several questions she should have asked.

Feeling confused and scared, Anna paid her money and pushed her way through the turnstile of the bus station. Don't get your hopes up, Hector Smythe had said. Well, she wasn't going to. Very soon the suspense would be over.

As the train hurtled its way through the tunnels she realised that part of the slightly sick feeling she was experiencing was due as much to low blood sugar as to the anticipation and fear of how she would acquit herself. It was past lunchtime and she had not eaten since eight o'clock, when she had had a small cup of coffee and a piece of toast. As soon as the appointment was over she would go into a café and get something to eat. If it was Simon, perhaps they could go together. She knew she could forgive him for disappearing from her life. He would have had good reasons, she felt instinctively, for the long silence.

Most likely she would not be in this situation if she did not need money to help raise her son. She would just have accepted that Simon was gone, even though his disappearance would have nagged at her for the rest of her life, and she dreaded future questions from her son about his father.

CHAPTER TWO

THE medical arts building was old and dignified, faced with pale stone, with dark oak panelling in the wide entrance hall. Stalling for time, with five minutes to go before her appointment, Anna stood in front of the directory of doctors that was displayed on the wall near the two lifts, as she rolled up her wet umbrella and unbuttoned her black trenchcoat.

Stay calm, she told herself sternly. You've come this far, so you've got to see it through. The worst he can do is tell you to go to hell, whether it's Simon or not.

With that, she got into a lift and pressed the button for the fourth floor, for Dr Ruelle's office, that he shared, according to the directory, with two others. The building had only four levels.

The fourth-floor corridor was hushed, the carpet thick as she silently walked along it, looking for the right office. In spite of her nervousness, she would go through with this. There was an inevitability about it now.

The receptionist in the public area of the office looked very sophisticated and sleek, serving to make Anna feel rather like a mouse that had fallen into a ditch full of water. Her leather shoes were damp, her hair windblown, while the attractive woman at the desk had not a hair out of place.

'I'm here to see Dr Ruelle,' Anna said softly, as she self-consciously pushed strands of her damp shoulder-length hair behind her ears. 'It's a…a personal matter,' she added that so the receptionist would not ask for her health card.

'Just along there,' the receptionist said, pointing along a short passage. 'Room three, at the end.' She did not ask for a health card or any proof of identity.

'Thank you.' Taking a deep breath, Anna let it out slowly, aware that she was gripping the handle of her shoulder-bag as though it were a lifeline.

Again the carpet was thick so that her footfalls made no sound as she walked slowly along the passage to room three, where the door stood open. Hesitantly, she waited on the threshold.

On the far side of the room, beside a window, a man was washing his hands at a sink, his back towards her. Her heart was pounding as she took in his appearance in those few seconds, the thick, dark hair with a tendency to wave slightly that was so like Simon's hair. This man wore a dark grey suit, almost black, well cut, which managed to emphasise the width of his shoulders and the powerful body that was above average height but not excessively tall. The first impression he gave, from back view, was one of strength. Simon had been like that.

She took a step into the room, swallowing to try to dispel the tightening of her throat. When he did not turn immediately, obviously unaware of her, she decided to speak.

Against all hope, she uttered the name. 'Simon?'

When he turned she could see that he was not Simon. Or was he? The colouring was the same, the pale skin contrasting with the dark hair, the blue-grey eyes, as were the square jaw and the firm, very masculine mouth. Could Simon have changed that much in the three years or so since she had last seen him? She did not think so. Also, this man was either a very good actor or he had never seen her before. There was no spark of recognition in his eyes as he looked at her from head to foot and back again.

'No, not Simon,' he said. He had a rather deep, gentle voice, pleasant. Not Simon's voice. 'Ms Grey?'

'Yes.'

Seth Ruelle looked at the young woman who stood before him, on the threshold of his office, at her pale face, her damp fair hair that fell to just above her shoulders, her blue eyes that had in them an expression of what he thought of as endurance.

She was thin and about five feet six inches tall. For some reason his interest quickened and he felt an unfamiliar sense of protectiveness, as though he could shield her from something that threatened her. It had been a long time since he had felt that certain softness for a woman. In fact, he did not recall ever having felt it to quite the same degree. This woman seemed totally unaware of how attractive she was, how she might affect a man. There was something very authentic about her, although he chastised himself for thinking that when he had only just set eyes on her and she had only uttered two words in his presence.

There were faint purple shadows under her eyes, and she looked tired and strained. Seth had the uncharacteristic desire to take her in his arms, to pull her head against his shoulder and stroke that pale hair that looked so fine and soft.

They stood staring at each other. Anna's heart was

pounding again with nervousness, with the shock of disappointment, and she felt sick. As she stared at the man in front of her she felt the blood draining from her face, light-headedness coming over her so that she stepped forward quickly and gripped the back of a chair.

'Are you all right?' he asked, coming towards her.

'No…I think I'm going to faint.'

In short order she found herself propelled forward, an arm round her shoulders, to sit in the chair. Then, as black spots floated before her eyes, she felt his hand on the back of her neck, pushing her head down to her knees.

'Keep your head down,' he said. 'That's right.'

He was back with a glass of water when she felt a little better, able to sit back in the chair, and he had closed the door. She knew that her lips were ashen, her face cold and stiff.

Dr Ruelle sat near her, not on the other side of the desk, as she sipped the water. 'You had better tell me what this is all about,' he said, looking at her astutely and curiously. 'I had a call from someone who said he was a private detective, with a client who was looking—urgently, he said—for a missing person. He said I might be able to help, but he declined to say how. It was very mysterious.'

Anna nodded wearily, thinking that she was wasting this man's time. 'I'm looking for a Dr Simon Ruelle, who has been missing…as far as I know…from Gresham, at least, for about four years.'

'Really?' He raised his eyebrows, looking interested. Dispassionately, Anna thought how attractive he was.

'Do you know him?' she enquired.

'No,' he said, looking at her thoughtfully and intently. 'Although he could be related to my family in some way. It's

not a common name and I don't know all the members of the
extended family. There have been a number of divorces, as
well as family feuds, I believe, that I don't know a great deal
about. Many of the extended family members are in Africa.'

'I'm sorry if I'm wasting your time,' she said, shifting un-
comfortably under his scrutiny. The exhaustion that she felt
must have shown clearly on her face. Now that her father was
ill, she was not looking after herself, and often forgot to eat.

'Tell me about it,' he said, not unkindly. For the first time
she was aware of his physical presence so close to her and,
surprisingly, she found herself drawing a certain comfort
from this stranger. He was, after all, a doctor, who should
have a measure of empathy.

'I'm trying to find the father of my child,' she said,
deciding not to prevaricate in any way, 'who disappeared. We
were not married. I tried to find him at the time but he seems
to have completely disappeared. He didn't know I was
pregnant, so I don't think he was running away from me. I
planned to tell him, then he vanished. I…only knew him
really well for about four months, although we'd worked
together for about six months before that, at Gresham
General, in the operating suite.' As she spoke, she did not look
at him. It all sounded a little sordid, she thought.

'You haven't told me your first name,' he said, leaning
towards her, with no particular inflexion in his voice, so that
she had no idea what he might be thinking.

'Anna,' she said. She was gradually feeling better.

'What do you want him for?' he asked. 'Is it money?'

Anna looked at him sharply, flushing. 'As a matter of fact,
yes, I am hoping for that,' she said, turning to look him full
in the face, finding an expression on his attractive features

that was unabashedly cynical. 'I'm struggling financially. But really that's not the main reason, it's almost incidental. I want my son to have a father, preferably his real father.'

As she spoke, she wondered whether she should add that she loved Simon, but that seemed too specious. Accordingly she was forced to confront the reality of whether she did still love the flesh-and-blood Simon, wherever he was, or just the idea of him as he had been when she had last seen him. Better to say nothing about that. Having to talk to this blunt stranger forced her to confront her own fears and realities.

When he continued to look at her, bending forward, his whole focus on her but saying nothing, she was forced to stumble on. 'You see I…I absolutely dread the day when my son will ask some serious questions about his father…which I think he will be doing soon. I would like to find Simon before my son starts full-time school.'

'So you haven't seen this guy in almost four years?'

'No…I mean, that's right.'

Seth Ruelle looked at his watch. 'You look as though you could use a good meal,' he said. 'I don't have much time, but I know a place nearby that we could walk to easily. You could give me the details then. I can't say I can help you, but I could make a few enquiries within the medical profession and among my lesser-known family members. If Simon is still practising medicine, he can be traced that way. I'm doing it because we have the same name, and I'm curious.'

'Thank you,' she said, standing up. 'I appreciate it very much.'

'Are you feeling all right now?' he asked, in a quietly so-licitous way, so that Anna had the strangely powerful feeling that she wished he would take her into his arms and hold her.

That was what loneliness did for you, she supposed, not having had male company when you needed it.

'Yes, thanks,' she said, gathering up her wet umbrella and her bag, trying to muster a certain dignity when she felt like the poor relation who had visited a wealthier family member to ask for money or shelter.

The restaurant was in an indoor shopping precinct, quiet and dimly lit, with charming ambience. Seating herself, Anna relaxed a little, having taken off her damp raincoat and hung it on a nearby hook. As she did so, Dr Ruelle looked at her again in an assessing way that was not particularly overt yet not surreptitious either, so that she felt a hot flush of self-consciousness.

In order to visit Hector Smythe, she had dressed in a turtleneck cashmere sweater in a purple colour that was flattering to her and a pale grey wool skirt, two of the nicer items that were in her rather meagre wardrobe. Now she was glad that she had taken the time to dress up a bit, as she knew those clothes suited her.

When the waiter came, she ordered a sandwich and a cup of coffee, deciding not to take up much more of this doctor's time. Already she was thinking that she was making a bit of a fool of herself with this stranger, who was not obliged to help her just because he had the same surname as Simon. Her thoughts bounced back and forth.

'I can give you half an hour, Anna,' he said. 'Start from the beginning.'

'Dr Simon Ruelle was a surgical fellow at Gresham General Hospital,' she began, as the waiter put her sandwich and coffee in front of her. 'We met because I was working as a nurse in the operating suite. We worked together a lot.'

'I see.' Seth wanted to reach forward and take her hand as she looked at him earnestly across the table, but he refrained, reaching for his coffee cup instead. Was she for real? he found himself thinking, his usual cynicism tempering the softness and increasing sexual attraction that he was feeling for this woman.

Hell, it wasn't as though he didn't have opportunities with women. Without being arrogant, he could truthfully say that he was being pursued more or less most of the time at work. And he did not want any of them, was unmoved by the overt advances. This young woman seemed not so much indifferent to his attraction as unaware of him as she frowned slightly at him and concentrated on her story. It was sobering, as well as disorientating to a certain extent. Usually he had often to be on the defensive with women.

'I suppose it was very naïve of me to become pregnant…but I did,' she said.

'How old were you when you met him?'

'I was twenty-two.'

'I think I was pretty naïve at twenty-two,' he said with a slight smile, which she supposed was to put her at ease. It was not easy talking about one's personal foibles and follies to a stranger.

'Go on,' he said.

'Simon disappeared before he had finished the fellowship,' she went on, her throat tight with nerves so that she could hardly get the words out. She would give him the story, try to convey the gamut of emotions, including shame, that she had felt at the time, the terrible anxiety and frustration.

'Because I had no claim on him whatsoever,' she went on, 'no one would talk to me about him, except in a very super-

ficial way. It was a matter of privacy for him, which I understand, of course. So I had difficulty in making enquiries of
my own, and because he'd been here for such a short time he
didn't have any really close friends who would otherwise
have told me what had happened to him.'

'You are certain he didn't know you were pregnant?'

'Yes, I'm certain. I went to see the chief of surgery, his
boss, early on, who said they didn't know where he was, but
if they did they probably wouldn't tell me because it would
be a breach of privacy.'

'Mmm. Go on.' He had ordered soup and a sandwich,
which he ate while he listened to her.

'I gave up trying to find him after a while.' She took a
swallow of the coffee and then a bite of her sandwich, forcing
herself to eat when she felt as though her throat had closed
up. Dr Ruelle seemed deep in thought, and the silence
between them was not strained.

'My parents helped me a lot,' she went on. 'I am very lucky
to have them to help me, although my father is now
ill…which is one of the reasons I want to find Simon.
He…should know he has a child…if he's still alive. I can't
help thinking that he might not be.' She bent over her plate,
not wanting him to see the fear in her eyes that she had dwelt
on for so long. 'I was able to go back to work three months
after the birth, and my mother looked after Finn, but now I've
given up again for the time being, until my father's well.'

'Finn—that's your son's name?'

'Yes.'

'A sweet name,' he said. Anna looked up, because his
voice had softened. When he smiled at her she felt, for the
first time, vulnerable to his attraction and his kindness.

Seth, looking at her closely, saw that change of expression in her eyes, that vulnerability and hint of awareness. It moved him, in spite of a holding back in himself.

'Do you have children?' Anna blurted out, not having planned to ask that.

'No,' he said.

Quickly she finished her food and coffee. 'Things changed just recently,' she hurried on, knowing that she only had a few minutes more of his precious time, 'because my father was diagnosed with prostate cancer, and my mother needs time to be with him.' There was no point in not telling him everything, she decided, as she had little time with him and he had to make up his mind whether he would help her. This might be her only chance. 'So, to be brief, I've decided to look for Simon again because I would appreciate some support—not just financial, but that, too.'

She wondered again what this stranger must be thinking of her. She didn't really care. He was a means to an end…or not, as the case may be.

'Will you have more coffee?' The waiter was there beside them, bearing a full coffee-pot, breaking into what was for her a rather awkward silence now. It wasn't often that she got to bare her soul like this. The events surrounding the birth of Finn had been kept confidential as far as possible, with only one or two friends at work having known about it when she had taken leave of absence.

'Yes, please,' she said. 'And could we have separate bills? We're ready for them now.' She did not want this Dr Ruelle to think that she was a freeloader, just because she needed help.

When she looked up at him, he had an expression of faint

amusement in his eyes. 'I'm beginning to be impressed by you, Ms Grey,' he said, with no further explanation.

'Good,' she said, feeling that she had to say something.

When the waiter had gone, her companion extended his hand across the table to her. 'My name's Seth, by the way. I didn't formally introduce myself before as I was concerned that you might collapse at my feet. Perhaps you knew it anyway?'

'Yes. How do you do?' she said, taking his hand.

'May I call you Anna?'

'Yes.'

'Has your father got a spread of tumour?' he asked, matter-of-factly.

'No, thank goodness,' she said. 'It was difficult, waiting for the pathology report.'

'Mmm, it always is.' He nodded. 'Tell me, did this Simon Ruelle indicate that he might be going out of town before he...er...disappeared?'

'Well, yes, he did. He told me that his mother had a home in Boston—one of several in various parts of the world, I think—and that she was ill and had been taken into hospital for an operation, that he was trying to get a few days off to go down to see her. We made a date for the following week after he got back, to have a meal together in a restaurant.'

'And he never showed up?'

'Right.'

'That should have been a definite lead, surely? Him being in Boston.'

'I tried to find his mother, but I didn't know her name. He had told me that his father had died, that she had married again and then divorced. He didn't tell me her name,' she explained. 'There was nothing to go on, you see.'

'Why would he not have contacted you?' He sipped his coffee, looking at her astutely over the rim of his cup. Uppermost in his mind was the thought that she ought to just let all this go, put it in the past and try to go forward. There was something very odd going on if this man had not contacted her in several years. If he were capable of doing so, and wanted to, surely he would have done so by now. Still, Seth refrained from telling her so, although the urge to do so was great. He couldn't really be critical, though, as he also allowed the past to influence him unduly, to keep him in a sort of emotional straitjacket.

'Something must have happened to him, something bad,' she said. 'That's been on my mind all this time. It's sort of driving me mad…'

'Someone must have reported him missing?'

'I don't know. We made a date to meet in our favourite small restaurant, on a specific evening, after he got back from Boston,' she explained, hearing the desperation in her own voice. That evening was something she would never forget. 'When he didn't come, I ordered a meal and a glass of wine…tried to make it last as long as possible.' While she had eaten that meal she had tried not to look at the door every few minutes, or the empty place-setting on the other side of the small table that was a mockery to her. Already feeling alone and vulnerable because of the pregnancy, his no-show had brought her situation home to her in full measure.

'That must have been very difficult for you,' Seth said softly. His empathy was almost palpable to her.

'When I called him on his cellphone,' she continued, 'there was only voice-mail. Then, eventually, even that stopped.'

Their second cups of coffee were finished and the waiter

had placed separate bills in front of them. Anna fumbled in her bag for her purse, her hands unsteady. Although it was a relief to articulate all this, it was also upsetting. Carefully, she counted out the money.

'Do you have a photograph of the missing man? And of your son?' Seth asked, his expression noncommittal, so that in spite of his obvious empathy and compassion Anna had no definite idea yet of whether he was really willing to help her.

'Yes, I do, I have them with me, because I had them copied for Mr Smythe, the detective,' she explained, 'and I had some extra ones printed.'

He took the two photographs that she handed to him, one of the handsome Dr Simon Ruelle, the other of her sweet, fair-haired son who smiled out of the picture with his innocent baby's eyes. Although Finn looked more like her than he did Simon, there was a definite resemblance between father and son. Indeed, there was a resemblance between Finn and the man sitting opposite her, which gave her a very odd feeling. Perhaps he, too, felt it.

'May I keep these for a while?' he said, looking at them intently.

'Yes,' she said, her dejected spirits lifting a little. That must mean he was going to help her in some way. 'I really appreciate the time you're giving me, Dr Ruelle.'

'I must get back. Give me your telephone number,' he said, passing her a notebook and pen.

They walked together to the exit of the precinct, where he drew her to one side. Resisting the urge to draw her into his arms, he decided to give in to the urge to speak his mind.

'Look, Ms Grey,' he said, speaking carefully, 'I have to tell you that I find your story somewhat…er…unlikely. I mean, what you say about your pregnancy not being known to this man. Please, don't take that the wrong way, as a criticism. It's not that I doubt the truth of what you have told me—certainly not that. I believe you. But perhaps he didn't need to be told that you were pregnant, he could probably see for himself, even if the pregnancy was not obvious to others and you were in the early stages.'

'It's possible, but not probable,' she said. 'I certainly didn't look pregnant at the time.'

'There could be several possible explanations,' he went on. 'Maybe he didn't want a child, didn't want to be married or living with a woman at that stage in his life, with his career just taking off. Maybe he didn't want to be tied down, period. It's possible that he thought you were not right for each other, child or no child. It's a common scenario. No offence intended.'

Anna caught her breath in distress, confronted by this now unsmiling man who had given the impression, albeit a slight one, that he believed her and felt a fair amount of empathy for her. Now he was telling her that he thought the basic premise of her story to be wishful thinking on her part, that she was wanting to find a man who did not want to be found by her.

'What you say may be true, but surely he did not have to disappear? I didn't necessarily want or expect him to marry me,' she said, flushing deeply, forcing the words out as her throat felt tight. 'I wanted him to know. You think I'm mis-construing everything?'

'Not necessarily, not all of it anyway. Perhaps you *are* deluding yourself to a certain extent. I think that your interpretation of the situation may be wrong.' He touched her arm. 'Look, I think he would have been stupid to have left you.'

That backhanded compliment left her more confused, to add to her upset. Perhaps he had just said that to soften the blow of his hard-headed take on the situation. 'I can understand how it might seem to you,' she said. 'But I knew him.'

Other people were coming in and out of the entrance. Through the glass doors they could see that the rain was heavier now. He took her arm and walked with her further out of the main path. 'Come.'

'You can't say,' he went on, 'that knowing someone really well…intimately, you might say…for only four months lets you know what they are all about. Perhaps he is, as they used to say in the old days, a bounder and a cad.'

'We worked together for longer than that. I felt that I knew him as well as anybody,' she protested.

'How well do we really know anybody when we are giving them what they want?' he said.

'You're very cynical.'

'You're an attractive woman, and I expect he was only too happy to have a relationship with you—at least, in the beginning. Who wouldn't?' he went on relentlessly.

'I—I'm sorry to have taken up your time,' she stammered, backing away a little from him, wanting to get out. 'It was good of you to see me. I know that what you say is common sense, but you don't know me and you don't know Simon. Perhaps I haven't explained very well, but everything I have said is true.'

'Perhaps it is, from your point of view,' he said. 'Forgive me if I seem cruel, I can only say how it seems to me. There are too many ifs and buts. The best thing you could do, Ms

Grey, is forget about him and get on with your life. Find
another man who will be a good father to your son.'

'I'm not going to do that, not until I know what happened
to Simon. That's not what I'm all about, and I don't need that
sort of advice, Dr Ruelle,' she said, anger helping her to save
face. 'I feel insulted that you should say that to me.'

'I'm sorry, Anna. That's how the picture seems. It's
realistic.'

'Then you can't help me to locate Simon?'

'I didn't say that. I don't think he will be too hard to find.
Have you considered that he might be married by now, with
other children?'

'No. Because I think something has happened to him.' She
faced him, embarrassed and hurt by what she saw as hostility,
and by the fact that her voice wobbled with emotion. 'Just in
case you think I didn't want the baby, I have to tell you that he
is the best thing that ever happened to me. Whether I find
Simon or not, I'll manage somehow, and I'll always adore my
son.'

An odd expression, quickly suppressed, had appeared on
Seth's face, something that she couldn't quite interpret at
that moment. It seemed like surprise and a certain vulnerability, as though he was used to hearing the opposite
sentiment expressed. Then she chided herself for speculating
about him. As far as she was concerned, he was a closed book,
and likely to remain that way. Nonetheless, in her desperation she decided to follow up on that moment of veiled
interest.

'I always wanted my child, before and after he was born,'
she said quietly, with dignity. 'Please, get that much straight,
Dr Ruelle. Neither did I become pregnant deliberately. I don't

expect you to help me in any way. Why should you? I met with you to make sure you were not Simon, to find out if you knew him, or of him. I certainly don't want anything from you. Thank you again, and goodbye.' She took a step back from him, feeling as though she wanted to cry. He was giving the impression now of being a hard man.

'Wait!' He stepped forward and caught her arm. To her surprise, he leaned forward quickly and kissed her on the cheek. 'I'll do what I can to find this Simon Ruelle,' he said curtly, 'but I may not necessarily tell you where he is. I'll decide that at the time, if it happens. My decision will depend on the circumstances. Your private detective will no doubt find it all out for himself, sooner or later.'

'You don't have to do anything,' she said, trying hard to control the tremble in her voice, nonplussed by his kiss, which probably meant nothing to him, she thought. Perhaps he was one of those men who went around kissing women he knew on the cheek 'I think I would prefer it if you didn't. As you say, I have the detective to do that.'

'We'll see,' he said, dropping her arm. 'I think you need help, in more ways than one. And I mean that in the nicest possible way. Goodbye, Ms Grey.'

'Goodbye,' she said stiffly, feeling as though she had come through a strange ordeal, which had left her feeling stunned. Part of the reason was that he was a very attractive man, and she had been increasingly aware of that fact while they had been together.

CHAPTER THREE

SETH went out ahead of her into the rain. When he had disappeared from view she followed slowly, putting up her umbrella, turning in the opposite direction.

She didn't want him to see her, to see the tears that were mingling with the few raindrops that had settled on her face, to see that the encounter with him had disturbed her much more than she had allowed to show. Not least, she had, in a strange sort of way, enjoyed having a meal with him. It had been a long time since she had eaten with an attractive man. Even though he was somewhat older than Simon, he was still young. That enjoyment showed her how much she really needed to have a man in her life, not to live the life of a cloistered nun, which was what it seemed like sometimes. Being a single parent was not exactly attractive to the opposite sex, she thought for the umpteenth time, unless perhaps some men thought she would be an easy sexual target, if they were of a predatory nature. For her part, she had become very discriminating.

It was not until she had turned a corner that she remembered the two photographs that she had left with him, which she would like to have returned.

That was probably the last she would see of them, because it was doubtful that she would have any further dealings with Dr Seth Ruelle.

Seth walked unheeding through the rain, his shoulders hunched. He didn't know what to make of Anna Grey.

Usually he felt more certainty when confronted with the opposite sex. At least, he had felt more confidence in his own judgement—based on mistrust and cynicism, it was true— since the debacle of his marriage and subsequent divorce. Perhaps he had been hard on her, but what he had said to her had been uppermost in his mind then, his take on the probable scenario of the doctor who had disappeared. He liked to tell the truth whenever possible. It was difficult to disappear unless one took on a totally new identity, and why would a doctor do that?

In spite of the sheer awfulness of the situation in his marriage, when he had found out the truth he had been oddly flattered subsequently that Belinda, the sophisticated, beautiful and accomplished Dr Belinda Dane, had been so determined to be his wife that she had woven a tissue of lies around her personal life in order to make sure that happened.

At first the marriage had been good, if perhaps, seen in retrospect, a little too good to be true. Belinda had gone out of her way to be a charming and compliant partner, striving to be good at everything she did where the marriage was concerned. Except, of course, in that one thing. He had been so blind. Sometimes it seemed to him that he had been wilfully blind. Perhaps that was partly why he now saw Ms Grey as deluding herself, and perhaps trying to delude him as well...although he did not think so.

Then later in his marriage when he had wanted to talk seriously about having a family, Belinda's subterfuge had inevitably come to the surface of their lives. He remembered the hard watchfulness of Belinda's eyes when she had tried to cover up her untruths, a memory which contrasted forcefully now with what he saw as hesitation and sadness in the shadowed eyes of Anna Grey.

Anna presented an endearing—he had to admit that—vulnerability mixed with a purely female strength, that the majority of women managed to find in themselves when protecting their children. Under his hard core of cynicism he had been touched by the way her face had lit up, her voice softened, when she had spoken of her child.

More disturbing, he had felt an unprofessional urge to cradle her in his arms when she had almost fainted in his office, and he had very much wanted her to accept the invitation to eat with him. She seemed totally unaware that she was attractive, as she was even when looking damp and starving. He could not find it in himself to repudiate her. Yet he would be careful, very, very careful.

He had a strong premonition that the missing Simon was distantly related to him, a descendant from the family that had split up in Zimbabwe in his grandfather's generation in a dispute over the ownership of land. It had been a bitter family feud, from what he had heard, a rift that had never been mended.

He felt that it had little to do with him—it had not had an impact on his life in any way. Some of the younger generations had gone into law and medicine, away from farming, so the ownership of land had receded into the past eventually. Some of the family, his own branch, had left Zimbabwe to set up in South Africa. Then some of his clan had decamped for North America and England, further disseminating the family ties.

As he walked away from Anna, his mind was engaged with her in a way that it had not been for a long time with a woman, an experience that left him amazed. He had withdrawn successfully from the opposite sex at an emotional level and he preferred it that way—at least, for the foreseeable future. Yet she had done nothing deliberately to make him engage with her in that way.

When she had looked at him he had been able to tell that she thought him an attractive man, yet felt herself removed from him in a personal way, as though she herself would have no impact on him and had no right to be involved with him in any way other than in the purpose for which she had come to see him.

In those few seconds when they had first made eye contact he had seen all this in her. He felt that she had summed him up, accurately and deeply. It had been a humbling experience. Then she had done nothing with it, had made no move towards him.

So often women gushed when they found him attractive, became overly talkative, sparkled in an effort to attract him. Usually he responded out of courtesy, not being a stand-offish person, feeling flattered as often as not, yet often otherwise unmoved. Once too often in his marriage he had been moved by flattery.

Now he wanted to turn round and hurry after her. He wanted to perhaps undo some of the things he had said that seemed harsh in retrospect. By now, she would be out of sight. At the very least he wanted to see her again. The thought occurred to him that perhaps his motives in his admonition to her to forget Simon and make another life for herself were ulterior. That insight also amazed him.

Yes, he told himself as he entered the medical arts building to go back to his office, as he tried to focus on his first appointment for the afternoon, he would proceed with caution where Anna was concerned. But he would proceed, nonetheless. That thought gave him a peculiar satisfaction.

'Mr Smythe? I'm afraid it was no go. Dr Ruelle wasn't Simon,' Anna said later on the telephone at home, then proceeded to give a precise explanation.

'No sweat,' the detective said cheerfully. 'It was a long shot, anyway. We've only just scratched the surface.'

'He may, or may not, help me,' she said. 'He asked for photographs of Finn and Simon, which I gave him.'

'Don't you worry. We'll track down Simon. Goodnight, Ms Grey. I'll be in touch.'

Going through the familiar routine later of preparing a simple evening meal for herself and Finn served to assuage the residual sadness that had been with her since the end of the long conversation with Seth Ruelle. It was as though his words had put a cap on her faltering hopes of finding Simon.

Yet her son, her family and her few close friends anchored her in a reality that allowed her to think that the world could also be a good and happy place. Very soon, when her father was fully healthy again, she would seriously look for part-time work. Already, a good friend of hers, Emma Fielding, who worked in the operating suite of University Hospital, the biggest teaching hospital in

Gresham, had told her that some vacancies might be coming up there.

'Do you want scrambled eggs, sweetheart?' she said to Finn, who was seated at their dining table, colouring with crayons in a book. In front of him on the table he had a toy farm with numerous animals, which he moved around from time to time.

'Yes.' Finn looked up at her and smiled, his love for her clearly on his face. Impulsively she put down what she was doing to go over to him to hug and kiss him.

'I like your picture,' she said. They were a mutual admiration society.

'Can I have ice cream after?' he said.

'Why not?' she said, kissing him again. It was so good to be with him. When she'd been at work he had always been on her mind, her longing to be with him sharp. Before having had Finn, she had not known or suspected what it was like to love a child, that overwhelming sense of adoration and protectiveness, that willingness to work and sacrifice for them.

They were in the basement apartment, she and Finn, of her parents' big old rambling house that they had bought many years before in a good residential area, at a time when there had been a slump in the housing market. Otherwise they could never have afforded such a house. Over the years they had slowly, painstakingly renovated and generally improved the house and gardens, doing a lot of the work themselves.

Anna broke eggs into a bowl and began beating them with a fork, considering yet again how fortunate she was to have this accommodation in her family home, to have parents who helped her in every way possible, as far as they could. Money was not plentiful, yet they managed to live with a sense of security most of the time. Just recently she had realised again that Simon should be in the picture. There were few real certainties in life.

Thoughtfully she stirred the eggs in a pot on the stove, then put Finn's portion on a plate, together with some vegetables.

'Here's your supper, darling,' she said. She lifted him into his booster seat at the table, tied a capacious napkin around his neck because he still made a mess when he ate but balked at having a bib tied round his neck, which he said was for babies.

'Mummy eat with me?' he said.

'Yes, I'm having an omelette,' she said.

As they ate, Finn talked about what he had been doing with his granny that afternoon, then what had happened at the play-group that he went to several mornings a week at the local small community centre.

The telephone rang when they were two-thirds of the way through their meal. 'Excuse me, sweetheart,' she said. 'I'll listen to the rest of the story later.'

She went into the kitchen to answer the telephone, from where she could still keep an eye on Finn but he could not hear precisely what she was saying. These days, since she had contacted the detective agency, she never knew when she might get a call from them.

'Ms Grey?' a deep, masculine voice enquired, pleasant and oddly soothing. It was not Hector Smythe. In spite of its pleasantness, she cringed a little inwardly, her heart seeming to make a disturbing flip of recognition that the owner of the voice was attractive to her. That was the last thing she wanted. 'This is Seth Ruelle.'

'Oh,' she said flatly. Although she had given him her number, she had assumed that it had just been a formality and that he would most likely not call her. Any information that he discovered about Simon he could pass on to Hector Smythe, she had also assumed.

'You don't seem overjoyed to hear from me, Anna...if I may call you that?' She could detect a faint amusement in his tone. For her part she felt more or less tongue-tied and was glad that he could not see her blush. Now that some time had elapsed, she felt that perhaps she should not have been quite so open with him about her private life and hoped that she would not regret it later.

'Er...do.' She said.

'I'm calling because my conscience has been bothering me,' he said. 'I may have seemed somewhat abrupt and rude today, for which I apologise. It goes against the grain.'

'You were a little...boorish, perhaps,' she conceded. 'But, as I said then, I was grateful for your time.'

'I like to think that I do not often forget my manners, pompous though that may sound,' he said.

'Especially not with a lady,' she finished for him.

This time he laughed. So he did have a sense of humour after all, she thought. Earlier in the day he had seemed, at the end of their conversation, somewhat suspicious and almost dour with her. Of course, she was a little paranoid, too, where her situation was concerned, somewhat on the defensive.

'Does that mean,' she asked, 'that you no longer find my story "unlikely", as I think you put it?'

Again he laughed. 'Sorry for that. Well...no, my views are more or less the same, essentially,' he said. 'It's just that I could have couched my remarks in more tactful terms. And, as I think I said, it's possibly your interpretation of events that might not be...er...in line with reality.'

'Yes, you could have put it more tactfully,' she said primly, disappointed that he had not fundamentally changed his stance. But perhaps she couldn't really blame him, when he knew next to nothing about her as a person. What she had divulged to him would obviously be in her favour.

'At the time,' he said, 'I felt it was probably better to be cruel to be kind.'

'Oh?' she said. 'You don't have to be kind, particularly, Dr Ruelle, especially if it's patronising, because I don't expect it. Neither do you have to be cruel. I think I understand my own situation pretty well, even though I am some-what…unrealistic, perhaps, and maybe given to wishful thinking. But thank you for calling. If you do find out anything, perhaps you would pass it on to Hector Smythe.'

'There is something else I want to tell you, Ms Grey,' he said. 'You said that you were looking for work, part time, so I wanted to let you know that there are positions available at University Hospital, in the operating rooms.'

'Do you work there?' she asked. During their conversation earlier in the day it had not come out where he worked, where he operated. She had just intimated that he was patronising, and here he was telling her about a possible job, which was good of him.

'Yes. It's a good place to work in. And I want to assure you that what you've told me will remain confidential,' he said.

'I had rather taken that for granted,' she said. It was a lie. At least he was sensitive to what she must be thinking, and she was pleasantly, though reluctantly, surprised. His somewhat contradictory attitude left her a little confused. 'I have a friend who works at University Hospital, in the OR— Emma Fielding. She told me there might be work soon.'

'Ah, yes, I know Emma. We work together a lot. Very good OR nurse.'

If she were to find employment at that hospital she could possibly be working with him if they were in the same service, and she did not want to start off on the wrong foot with a verbal sparring match. Her antipathy matched what she sensed in him, which was not to women *per se*, for she felt that he found her attractive, in spite of himself, but to trusting and getting involved. How she knew that, she could not say. It came from a sort of instinct. Having thought that, he might be married for all she knew, even though he had said he had no children.

She and Simon had loved each other passionately and completely in the short time that they had known each other, and in that time she had learnt a lot about human relation-ships, about being really close to someone emotionally, spiri-tually. That was why she was so convinced that something awful had happened to him.

With this man, Seth Ruelle, she sensed a desire for close-ness, yet a rigid holding back. Again, how she knew that, she could not have said. In her job she had to know something about human nature, as he did in his. It was evident that he did not trust her, or he did not trust her judgment—he had made that much clear, something which his apology did not annul.

'Um, what sort of surgery do you do?' she enquired.

'General surgery,' he said. 'With an interest in the liver.'

'Transplants?'

'No. Although I do assist with transplants frequently, to keep my hand in. I mainly remove parts of diseased livers.'

'That's interesting,' she said, forcing herself to speak

calmly when she found herself somewhat disturbed, and not sure why. 'I worked in the general surgery service in the operating suite myself, at Gresham General.'

'Mummy!' Finn shouted, loud enough for Seth to hear.

'You must be busy,' he said.

'Um…yes. I must go. I would like to get the two photographs back from you, too, please, Dr Ruelle.' As she said his name, she thought again how odd it seemed to be saying Simon's name. No wonder she felt disturbed.

'Of course,' he said smoothly. 'So you accept my apology, Ms Grey?'

'Oh… Yes, I do, Dr Ruelle. Thank you.'

'Mummy! I want to get out of my chair,' Finn yelled.

'I must go. Goodnight and…er…thank you again.' She hung up.

'Wait, Finn,' she said, rushing into the sitting room. 'You haven't had your ice cream yet.'

'All right,' he said, settling back into his chair.

'I won't be a minute,' she said.

As she took out two cartons of ice cream from the freezer and took them into the sitting room with a glass dish, she thought again how odd it was that she had had very little meaningful personal contact with men since Simon had gone. Although she had worked with many men as part of the large OR team, that had all been very professional. The short time she had spent with Seth had made her even more acutely aware how much she missed male company. It left her with a hollow sense of mourning. She had not allowed herself to be available or respond to the vibes of other men.

Emma had never met Simon, as he had worked at Gresham General. She, Anna, had told Em something about Simon in general terms, but did not think she had told her his surname. At the time, she had wanted to keep her personal affairs very private. If Emma had known his name, she would, no doubt, have said something when Seth had started work at University Hospital. It was just as well, less complicated, that few people should be in a position to connect the two individuals.

'Chocolate or vanilla?' she said to Finn, giving him another kiss on the forehead. 'Or some of each?'

'Each,' he said.

'So it shall be.'

Her parents' part of the house was spacious, filled with cosy clutter—lots of books and pictures, comfortable furniture, eclectic knick-knacks—and she looked forward to taking Finn up there for a short while in the evenings after supper.

Although Finn did not have a father that he knew, he had a grandfather who loved him. Finn called his grandfather Poppa. Anna had kept a photograph of Simon in the sitting room from Finn's birth, so he knew what his father looked like, and he didn't question her explanation that his father was away somewhere. Too young to understand, he just accepted as normal that his father could not be with them.

Anna and Finn, holding hands, went up the basement stairs to her parents' kitchen. As they reached the top of the stairs and saw her father sitting at the kitchen table, Finn ran forward, calling 'Poppa! Poppa!'

'How's my boy?' Her father smiled, holding out his arms.

Looking at them, Anna knew that she must persist in trying to find Simon. Sometimes her resolve in that faltered, especially earlier today when Seth had cast doubts on her own perceptions. In spite of him, she must go on. Once Finn started proper school he would see that other children had fathers. In the meantime, "Poppa" was a great father.

Statistically, Seth had a point, a very strong one, she had to admit. Some men, no doubt, would be willing to give up a job, a good training position, in order to escape from a woman they did not want to be with. She had seen that knowledge and cynicism in his eyes as he'd looked at her. She had also seen it, veiled, in the more experienced eyes of Hector Smythe. It was nothing personal, she knew that—it was simply an acceptance of common fact, of human nature.

Sweet Simon, a man of integrity, she knew, did not come into that category.

She kissed her mother and gave her a hug. 'How are you?' she asked. 'And how's Dad? He looks good.'

'He is good, and I'm all right. Not quite as frazzled as I was before Dad's operation.'

'Good. Mum, I'm thinking of applying for a job at University Hospital. I've heard from my friend, Emma, that there's work, part time, in the OR. Is that all right with you? Will you be able to babysit again?'

'I don't see why not, once your dad is fully operational again.'

'I'm going to phone Emma and ask her to get me an application form from the human resources department, then I'll have to go for an interview with the head nurse of the department,' Anna said. 'If they take me on, I could be working in about two weeks.'

Lying in bed, sleepless, later that night, she found that she could not get Seth Ruelle out of her mind, and the fact that he had phoned her. That had been unexpected. She thought of his thick, dark hair, which looked as though it would be soft to the touch, and she acknowledged that she would like to run her fingers through it. Today he had been largely un-smiling as he had looked at her, taking in her story, assessing her. She would like to see him smile more, just at her…

CHAPTER FOUR

THE hospital did take her on, to work Mondays, Wednesdays and Fridays.

First, there was a two-week orientation period, during which she was paired with her friend and colleague, Emma, under a 'buddy system' that they had in place for new personnel.

On the first day of the orientation period, she planned to meet Emma in the locker room where the OR nurses changed from their outdoor clothing to the scrub suits and white shoes that they wore for the job.

'Hi, Anna!' her friend called to her, and waved from the far side of the locker room when she entered, rather tentatively.

The place was packed with nurses changing quickly in order to get a cup of coffee before having to go on duty. The level of chatter was deafening.

She knew that although they did not officially have to start work until half past seven, most nurses got there at seven, or before, so that they could start on their work early. There was a lot to do to prepare for the first case starting sharply at eight, although the night nurses did much of the prep. Just opening the large sterile packs of instruments and drapes took quite a lot of time. Then the nurse who was to "scrub" for the case had to go through the scrub process, organise her work tables of sterile instruments and count the sponges and instruments if there was to be an open body cavity, as there was in major general surgery.

As she made her way through the crush of bodies towards the locker that was hers, beside Emma's locker, her mind ranged swiftly over all that, over the familiar routine. The sense of excitement, tinged with stress, took hold of her. That was also familiar, an occupational hazard. The time to worry was when you didn't feel stress, when you relaxed too much and let your concentration drop. That was when things happened that shouldn't happen.

'This is Anna Grey, everyone!' Emma yelled over the sound of conversation.

'Hi, Anna!' There was a general chorus of welcome. They were a good crowd, so Emma had told her.

'Welcome to University Hospital OR,' someone said. 'The only place to be in the whole city. You want something replaced, taken out, lifted or shifted, this is the place to be.'

There was general laughter. 'Thanks,' Anna said, smiling all round. Already she liked the ambience of the place.

'I got you a scrub suit,' Emma said, handing her a pale blue two-piece cotton suit. 'You've got your shoes with you?'

'Yes, thanks.'

'We're going to be working together in the general surgery service, as I told you on the phone the other day. That hasn't been changed. And…' She lowered her voice. 'It's Dr Ruelle today in our service.' Anna had told her about meeting Seth Ruelle, and something about the circumstances of their meeting.

'OK,' Anna said, her stress level going up a few notches. She was missing Finn, whom she had left with her mother.

'There will be three of us in the room today, as it's your orientation period,' Emma went on, as she took off her outdoor shoes. 'You'll scrub with me for the first case, mainly observing, which is for a partial removal of liver, for an early stage metastatic cancer.'

'I see,' Anna said, hanging her coat in the locker.

'There are three rooms in the general surgery service, and we'll be working in one of them,' Emma said. 'We'll grab a cup of coffee before we go in. Never pass up an opportunity to take some nosh in this place.'

Once changed, they headed out at a quick walk to go to the coffee-lounge that was just for the doctors and nurses who worked in the operating suite. Feeling a little shy, Anna followed Emma and did what she did.

'What's he like to work with, this Dr Ruelle?' Anna asked, when they were standing together, nursing their Styrofoam cups of coffee.

'Pretty good,' Emma said ruminatively. 'He's a nice guy, if a little reticent at times. He's gorgeous, really, in every respect.'

'Yes, he's very attractive,' Anna admitted.

'If I were not so besotted with Ross,' Emma said, referring to her boyfriend, 'I could fall for Seth Ruelle in a big way.' She laughed. 'No one knows much about his private life. Mind you, that's not a bad thing when you think of the gossip around here. Don't give anyone food for thought, that's my motto. Anyway, he hasn't been here long, less than a year. Came from somewhere in the States. He's an asset to our place. Before he came, there was no one who specialised exactly in what he does with the livers.'

'Does he know I'm coming?' Anna said.

'He knows,' Emma said. 'I told him.'

Anna let out her breath on a sigh of relief. It was going to be a rather strange situation. The best thing, she had decided, was not to let anyone know, other than Emma, that she had ever set eyes on Dr Seth Ruelle before that day. No one else in this hospital knew anything about her private life.

Inside the inner sanctum of the operating suite proper, the porters were wheeling in patients on stretchers, to park them in front of their designated rooms. Rooms one, two and three were for the general surgery service.

There was another nurse in room one when they went into the general surgery unit. 'Hello, Jay,' Emma said to her. 'This is Anna Grey. She'll be scrubbing with me. Anna, this is Jemimah, otherwise known as Jay.'

'Hi,' Jay said, coming forward to shake her hand. 'Pleased to meet you, and welcome to the team. I'll be the circulating nurse for the first case. It's great to have you with us.'

'Hi. Good to be here.'

'If you could just open up the gown pack and put out the gloves, Em,' Jay said, 'I'll do the rest.'

'Sure.'

The anaesthetist for the room came in then. 'Hi, girls. How are you?' he said, tying a disposable face mask over his nose and mouth. He was wearing the usual green scrub suit.

'Pretty good, thanks,' Jay said. 'We have a new nurse, Dr Jarvis. This is Anna Grey…Anna, this is Ray Jarvis.'

They shook hands. He was middle aged, grey-haired, and looked exhausted. 'Welcome to the team,' he said. Then he began to check his complex anaesthetic machine, which would administer anaesthetic gases and oxygen to the patient.

'Come on,' Emma said to Anna, when she had opened the gown pack and put out latex gloves for them and the surgeons. 'Let's go out and get scrubbed. You can meet Dr Ruelle out there.'

The scrub sinks were immediately outside the door to the room, each operating room having its own set of sinks. As they went out, she saw Seth talking to his patient who was on a stretcher near the sinks, and the sight of him made her feel incredibly uptight, as though he would somehow be judging her. She also felt an unwelcome pull of attraction. Unwelcome because she didn't know how to deal with it. There was an inscrutability about him. Immediately he raised a hand in greeting to them and excused himself from the patient.

'You know Anna, Dr Ruelle,' Em said, making her voice sound formal. 'This is her first day.'

'Yes,' he said quietly, holding out a hand, his eyes searching her face—what was visible of it behind the face mask and the soft paper hat that covered every bit of her hair. 'Congratulations on getting the job, Anna. Quite a coincidence that we should find ourselves here. Welcome, and I hope you enjoy working here.'

'Thank you,' she said, taking his hand and looking, briefly, into his astute blue-grey eyes that looked back at her as though he could see into her soul. His hand was warm and firm. Although his words were welcoming, he did not smile. For her part, she hoped that he could not sense how attractive she found him, in spite of her ambivalence towards him. His somewhat cutting words at their first meeting were very prevalent in her mind.

'And how are you, Emma?' he said, letting go of Anna's hand, his tone taking on a lighter note.

'Very well. We'll both be scrubbing for you,' Emma said.

Anna turned away, determined then and there to keep a low profile, if she could, where Seth Ruelle was concerned.

The two nurses started the scrub process, then before long the anaesthetist and Jay came out to wheel the patient into the room. 'See you in there,' Seth said to his patient, a middle-aged man, touching him briefly on the shoulder.

Anna already understood, from what she had observed in the last few minutes, that Seth had a good rapport with his patients, that he had empathy and compassion, a good bedside manner, good communication skills. Those were attributes that were not as common as one might imagine, she speculated. People went into medicine for different reasons, she knew that, so it was idealistic to suppose that they all had the human quality of empathy that was so vital. Almost reluctantly she found herself warming to him.

At the same time she felt a sense of dissonance as she heard others refer to him by his name, and instantly had visions of Simon, the other Dr Ruelle, who had been at Gresham General. The frustration of not knowing where he was assailed her again.

Tactfully, Emma went ahead of her into the operating room, leaving her alone with Seth, who had started the scrub process at the sink beside her. Emma had probably sensed that they would like to have a few words with each other.

'Take your time, Anna,' Emma said, as she left them.

His presence made her feel gauche somehow, and she wondered what he thought of her, a young woman who had entered into a sexual relationship with a colleague she had known only a short while. Then she had become pregnant in this day and age when it was relatively easy to avoid pregnancy.

There was no way that she could explain it adequately herself, except that they had loved each other, that there had been a rare rapport that she, for one, had never experienced before. Now, subdued by circumstances, she could not always understand her own earlier behaviour. From the perspective of time passing, she could see now that what had seemed extraordinary to her must seem commonplace to an observer…like Seth Ruelle, for instance.

'Have you,' he said, looking at her sideways, 'had any other word from the private detective since I last spoke to you?'

Quickly she glanced at him and away again, feeling unaccountably shy. Perhaps that was because he knew too much about her in some ways, and in other ways not enough.

'He has called me twice,' she said, 'just to tell me that he's pursuing some leads, and not to get discouraged.'

'And are you discouraged?' he asked quietly.

'I… Well…I do feel somewhat depressed about the whole thing,' she admitted thoughtfully. 'And, yes, I think you could say that I feel discouraged—because so much time has elapsed.'

'Mmm,' he said.

'Working with you, another Dr Ruelle,' she blurted out, 'makes me feel very…strange, to say the least.'

'Then you must call me Seth, when we're out of the actual operating room,' he said. 'Seth sounds very different from Simon.'

'All right. Thank you,' she said.

Two other young male surgeons joined them at the scrub sinks. Seth introduced them to her as the senior surgical resident-in-training and the surgical intern. That put an end to their conversation.

Then she left him to go into the operating room, to dry her hands on a sterile towel, put on a sterile gown and a pair of sterile latex gloves.

Emma was already making good progress in setting up the instrument tables for the case.

'What can I do?' Anna said to her.

'First, you can help Dr Ruelle put on his gown and gloves,' Emma said. 'Then I'll get you to open some of the suture packets and mount the needles on needle-holders. You can be responsible for those during the operation.'

'OK,' Anna said, going over to the gown table to wait for Seth to come in so that she could hand him a towel, then open up the gown.

Seth…Seth…I must think of him as Seth. She repeated the name to herself silently, over and over again. It was the duty of the scrub nurse to hold open the gown for the surgeon so that he could put his arms into the sleeves, then she would hold open each glove so that he could put his hand into it without touching the sterile outside part. She felt reasonably calm now, her knowledge of the familiar routine coming back to her with ease.

It was inevitable, being in an operating room again, that she would think of Simon. Even as she thought that, she could almost hear the cynical voice of Hector Smythe saying, 'It always does seem natural,' or words to that effect, when she had spoken of their love seeming right for them.

It had only been later, after Simon had disappeared, that she had been forced to consider their different backgrounds, that he came from a different social background from the one that she had come from, that perhaps he would not wish to marry her for that reason. And she had thought of marriage with him, in all her naïvety, she had to admit that to herself.

'Thank you, Anna,' Seth said to her as she dutifully handed him a towel.

Thoughts of Simon disappeared as she found herself very aware of this flesh-and-blood man who stood close beside her, of his broad shoulders, his powerful presence. He seemed to exude a quiet, confident manliness that came naturally to him. It served to make the memory of Simon, who seemed like a wraith then, existing in her imagination only, fade somewhat like an old photograph that had been exposed too much to the light.

'Let me tell you something about this patient,' he said very quietly, 'so that you can be prepared, Anna, as we may get into a blood-clotting problem with him. I've already told Emma about it.'

'All right.' Anna nodded.

'Some years ago he had hepatitis C, which damaged his liver, leading to cirrhosis. That doesn't show up right away after the acute infection, it takes time to develop. Now he has a cancer of the liver, a primary tumour, which is quite common in people who have cirrhosis. Fortunately, it's only confined to one lobe, which we can remove. That's what we're going to do this morning. A cirrhotic liver is usually very vascular, with engorged veins, so we have one problem there.'

'I see,' she said. This was going to be an interesting case.

'Because the liver has been damaged,' Seth went on, 'our patient has problems with blood clotting. That is, it does not clot as efficiently as it should do. I expect you know the detailed physiology of the blood-clotting mechanism?'

'Something,' she said. 'I'll certainly look it up to refresh my memory when I get home tonight.'

'I won't go into all that now. For us, today, the implications are that we have to be prepared for excessive haemorrhage during the operation, even though we've given him blood transfusions, with whole blood and blood platelets,' he said. 'We may need to renew those during the operation.'

'I understand,' she said.

'Just as well I'm going to have two scrub nurses,' he said, smiling. 'We'll need a lot of sponges, and probably more ties and sutures than usual.'

'I'll be ready,' she said. While nervous, she felt herself gearing up to meet the challenge, and she would have Em with her, who would be the primary scrub nurse.

'I'm sure you will,' he said.

When he was gowned and gloved, the other two surgeons came in and she went through the same process with them.

Their patient had a new intravenous line in place, two in all, put there by Dr Jarvis, and when Seth had had a few reassuring words with him he quickly became unconscious as Ray Jarvis injected the anaesthetic drugs into one of the intravenous lines.

They all waited quietly for their patient to be intubated. Then, before too long, the operation was under way, the skin prepped, the patient's body covered with sterile drapes.

'We've got extra sponges,' Em said to Anna, in a whisper, 'because of the possible heavy bleeding. We'd better take that as a given. Maybe you could help me keep track of the sponges, Anna, as well as dealing with the ties and the sutures. OK?'

'Sure,' she said. Quickly she began to organise her sutures in the packages in the order that they would be needed.

There were a few seconds of quiet. 'Are we ready, Emma, Anna?' Seth said.

'Ready.'

Seth looked at Emma. 'Knife, please, Emma,' he said.

CHAPTER FIVE

ANNA concentrated totally on the job, methodically tearing open small packets of suture material, mounting each needle on a needle-holder in the order in which they would be used.

'Fortunately for our patient,' Seth explained, 'the tumour is relatively small and confined to one lobe of the liver. Just as well, because this cancer is compounded by the severity of the liver damage from the cirrhosis that I was telling you about.'

Anna nodded. Jay had given her a long, flat stool to stand on, which gave her a good view of what was going on inside the abdominal cavity. At the same time she could watch very closely what Emma was doing. There was nothing out of the ordinary about this operation—it was not fundamentally different from any other major abdominal case—and Anna anticipated that before very long she would be scrubbing for Seth on her own.

Only once did her mind wander for a few seconds, and that was when she thought of the first time she had scrubbed for Simon. He had explained what he had been doing, without talking down to her, even though she had been familiar with the gut resection operation that he'd been engaged on. Then, when the operation had ended, he had taken her aside to thank her personally for her calm and competent assistance, as he had put it.

She had grinned back at him. When he had taken off his mask and smiled at her, she had been instantly in love. From then on he had smiled at her a lot. It had not been long before they had gone out to dinner together. Then they had held hands in a movie, like two young teenagers. It had all been so innocent and sweet. They had not planned to sleep together, to get really involved—it had happened, seemingly as inevitable as the rising sun.

Again the image of Simon faded from her mind.

As Seth was part way through the procedure, the excessive bleeding started. 'As you can see,' Seth said, for the benefit of the surgical intern and Anna, 'there is a lot of scarring and fibrous tissue in a cirrhotic liver. The lobes are not as clearly defined as they would be in a non-cirrhotic liver.'

Anna and the intern, John, both nodded as they stared into the abdominal cavity. There was collective added tension and alertness among all of the staff. 'Extra sponges, Emma,' Seth said. 'Ready with the suction, Ben.' Emma had already anticipated his needs, as any good scrub nurse did.

Anna opened another bundle of large gauze sponges and counted them with Emma. They came in bundles of five, every sponge having to be counted and recorded lest it be left behind by mistake in the abdominal cavity. Ben, the surgical resident, became more active in suctioning blood with a suction tip and tubing attached to an electrical pump mounted on the wall. Blood ran into a clear receptacle, calibrated so they could see clearly the amount of blood loss in millilitres from that source.

'Jay, would you get me a bag of whole blood and one of platelets from the cooling cupboard, please?' Dr Jarvis asked their circulating nurse, gearing up to deal with the bleeding crisis. He was the one who would have to keep the patient hydrated and alive during the operation.

'Sure,' Jay said, going out of the room. The cooling cupboard was just outside in the corridor, containing bags of blood which had already been typed and cross-matched for specific patients who were being operated on that day. Very quickly she was back, carrying the bags of blood. Before long, the bags had been mounted on the intravenous poles, connected to the IV tubing, and were dripping blood into their patient's veins.

Anna felt tense as she watched blood soaking up into the sponges that she was handing up to the surgeons and the blood that was being sucked into the plastic container.

'I'd like some catgut ties, Anna,' Seth said to her, 'then give me a fine black silk suture.' Although Seth was calm, she could hear the tension in his voice. 'I want to do a bit of sewing here before I continue dissecting. Ben, would you grab the catgut with the tip of artery forceps? I want to tie off some of the bleeders.'

Anna had the appropriate suture ready, mounted on a long metal needle-holder. Quickly she handed it up to Seth when he had finished the catgut ties, and then she made sure that she had another ready of the same type.

Apart from the sporadic verbal requests, the sighing of the anaesthetic machine, as it transferred gases to their patient and took them away again, and the sound of the suction, all was quiet in the room, no noises from outside penetrating.

Time moved quickly, yet also seemed to stand still, as they

fought to control the massive bleed. Anna thought of it as a sort of battle. Ray Jarvis, very calm, manipulated the various bags of intravenous fluids and blood that he was giving to their patient. Carefully, expertly, and as swiftly as possible Seth continued to dissect out the lobe containing the tumour and sew up and tie blood vessels at the same time to control the bleeding.

Jay dropped more bundles of sterile sponges onto their sterile set-up, then waited while they counted them. It was Jay's job to record all the sponges, instruments and needles that they were using, one of her many jobs as the circulating nurse.

When the lobe of the liver, with the tumour in it, was finally lifted out, there was another surge of blood which they had to stem, even though Seth had carefully tied off and sewn up bleeding vessels as he'd gone along.

When the operation was finished and their patient transferred to a stretcher to be wheeled to the recovery room, Anna felt drained and somewhat tremulous. There were blood-soaked sponges on sheets and on the floor, where they had been counted, and the plastic bottle on the wall was almost full.

'Thank you, everyone,' Seth said, taking off his surgical gloves and throwing them into a waste bucket. 'That all went as it should, given the circumstances. We'll take a coffee-break, all of us, of at least twenty minutes.'

Just as Anna was gazing around the room at the mess of bloodstained linen and used instruments and equipment, thinking that it would take them more than twenty minutes to clean up and prepare for the next case and that they would not get a coffee break, two relief nurses came into the room.

'Coffee-break, girls,' one of them said, bright and breezy. 'You look as though you could use one. We'll do the clearing up.'

'Thanks, girls,' Emma said. 'We sure could use it. Come on, Anna, get that gown off before they change their minds.'

In the staff coffee-lounge, Anna followed Emma, picked up a cup and filled it from one of the urns, adding cream and a generous portion of brown sugar.

'Ah, I've been longing for this,' she said to Emma, as they moved out of the way to stand against a wall, all seats having been taken for the moment.

When Seth came into the room a moment later, she found herself tensing, very aware of his presence, thinking again of what he had said to her when they had first met. Obsessively, she could not get it out of her mind, feeling that he did not trust her. When he came over to her, bearing a full cup of coffee, she tensed even more, hoping he planned to talk to Emma.

Instead, he gave her his full attention and she felt her cheeks warming. 'You were great in there, Anna,' he said, 'obviously a very good and experienced OR nurse, who is going to be a great asset to this department. Thank you again. I was very impressed.'

'Thank you. You're making me blush,' she said, quite unnecessarily, as he was clearly noting her flushed face.

'Good,' he said, grinning at her and Emma. 'It makes me feel young again to find a woman who can blush at what I have to say to her.'

'Get on with you,' Emma said scathingly. 'You are young.'

'I'm thirty-five, going on fifty.'

'That's nothing,' Emma said. 'I'm twenty-seven, going on fifty.'

Distractedly, Anna thought her own thoughts. It's not just what you say that makes me blush, she thought tartly, it's also what you know about me and what you can infer from what I've told you. Biting her tongue, she refrained from articulating her thoughts. Maybe if Emma had not been there, she would have said something of her thoughts, if not all.

In the crowded room he stood close, of necessity, and she felt overwhelmed. 'It…it was a very interesting case,' she said. 'Will he be all right?'

'He'll get over the operation all right,' he said. 'But he's not out of the woods, of course, having had cancer. There does not seem to be a spread of the tumour, so when he's recovered we may give him a course of chemotherapy to make sure he's all right on that score.'

'I see.' Anna nodded. 'I do hope he'll be all right, he's still young.'

'Yes, he's only forty-four.'

They continued to talk, while Anna felt her red cheeks gradually returning to normal, and Emma tactfully left them to get herself another cup of coffee.

And I'm very impressed with you, Seth Ruelle, Anna thought, very, very impressed. In some ways she felt as though she had been knocked over by a sledgehammer, that was the effect he was having on her. It was pathetic really, she chided herself, the first good-looking, charming man you come into contact with, you turn into a quivering jelly because you've been deprived for so long. Tensely, she wondered if he could divine something of her reaction to him, hoping fervently that it was not the case. After all, she knew next to nothing about him. He might be married, and have a harem on the side as well. She smiled at her own feeble joke.

'Can I share the joke?' he said, looking at her quizzically.

'Oh, no,' she said. 'A very private thought.'

'Pity. Can I get you another cup of coffee, then? That will give you a chance to get those lovely cheeks to stop burning.'

'It's cruel of you to remark on it,' she said.

'I know,' he said, taking her cup out of her weak hand. 'Don't take any notice of me. It's a while since I've enjoyed anything that approximated a flirtation.'

'Is that what it is?' she said. 'The same goes for me, so I can't even recognise one.'

He grinned at her. 'Don't go away, Ms Grey,' he said.

I wouldn't dream of it, she thought. For one thing, her legs were so weak she couldn't walk. And another thing—she had an excuse in the shape of a child for not having had a flirtation. She wondered what his reasons could be. That didn't go with the harem idea.

'You look bemused and somewhat glassy-eyed,' Emma observed as she sidled up to Anna. 'I'm going to the washroom before going back, and I advise you to do the same, but not before you've had a good old flirt with the delectable Seth.'

'Oh, God, is it noticeable?'

'Only to me, as I'm highly attuned to those things, and I know him pretty well. I would say that he's dying to get his hands on you.'

'Oh, Em. Don't say that. I can't live with it.'

'I have said that.'

'Is he…is he married?' she whispered urgently.

'Not that I know of,' Emma said, 'but I bet he's got a lot on the side.'

'I was thinking that he might have a harem.'

'That too,' Emma said. They both laughed.

'He's attractive,' Anna conceded. 'But I don't even like him. He was rather mean to me when I met him.'

'Sure you like him. It's all over your face.'

'Oh, is it? Heck!'

'Don't worry, that's only because I know you well. Nobody else could tell. Here he comes, so I'm going. Don't forget that washroom. You might find yourself standing for the next four hours, unable to leave the room.'

'What has she been saying to you?' Seth enquired as he handed her the coffee. 'She likes to tease.'

'She suggested that you had a harem,' Anna dared to say, putting words into Emma's mouth, then took a swallow of the too-hot coffee.

'And she said that I was planning to add you to it?'

'Well…something like that,' she said, flushing again.

'She might be right there,' he said.

Anna looked at the big clock on the wall, seeing that she had only four minutes left of the coffee-break. 'Oh, time's up,' she said. 'I must go back.'

Seth grinned at her. 'Running away from me, Anna?'

'Yes,' she said. With the cup gripped firmly in her hand, she let herself out of the lounge and strode along the outer corridor towards the washroom. She had almost forgotten the extent of the friendly joking and teasing that went on in the operating rooms, to defuse the tension of the job. It generally didn't mean anything, and one took it in the spirit in which it was intended. Seth's flirtations, if one could call them that, did not mean anything.

Emma was coming out of the washroom.

'See you back in the OR,' Emma said. 'Do you want to

scrub with me for the next case? It should be a straightforward removal of a lobe of the liver, no cirrhosis, for a secondary tumour. We're running late now, of course.'

'Yes, I'd like to scrub, Em.'

After the stress of the previous case, she now felt light and optimistic, basking in the praise that Seth had given her. It had been generous of him.

CHAPTER SIX

THE rest of the day went by quickly, an interesting day all in all. When the evening shift of nurses came on duty at half-past three, Dr Ruelle was just finishing his last elective case of the day.

'Thank you, Emma,' he said quietly. 'Thank you, Anna. I hope it's been a good first day for you.'

'Oh, it has,' Anna responded enthusiastically. 'Very interesting.' What she really wanted to say was that she had found him very impressive, his technical skill, his calm assurance and his polite interaction with everyone he worked with…which was not the case with all surgeons. But there was no way she could say that.

'Great. I'll look forward to working with you again,' he said. 'Will it be Wednesday?'

'Yes,' she said.

Unlike Simon, he did not rip off his mask theatrically in front of her. Instead, he looked at her steadily, seriously, his joking mood of the coffee-lounge gone, as though he was trying to suss her out, which had an odd, disturbing effect on her. Just by working together, in this tense atmosphere, they were certainly getting to know something about each other. In a place like this there was no subterfuge.

The evening shift nurses came into the room then, breaking the emotional contact that had temporarily sprung up between Anna and Seth in the brief verbal exchange and eye contact.

As she turned to go out of the room, Anna remembered the words that he had uttered when he first met her. 'I find your story unlikely.'

She tried to harden her heart against him.

It was good to have a day off after each day of work, in which she could catch up on all the things she had to do of a domestic nature and spend time with Finn.

On the Friday of that first week she scrubbed for the first case of the day on her own, Emma and Jay having decided that she was ready and she had agreed.

Although she was nervous, she felt that she would be all right, with Emma there to keep a watchful eye on her and to prompt her if necessary. One of the more difficult things was to remember all the different sutures that the surgeons used to sew up and to close the incision. She took deep, calming breaths while they were waiting to commence.

When Seth had carefully and expertly removed the liver tumour he'd been operating on and had placed it in a stainless-steel bowl, he turned to Jay, the circulating nurse. 'Jay, would you ask the pathologist to come here to take a look at this, please? She's expecting my call. Before I close up here, I want to make sure the margins are clear.'

Anna knew that the pathologist would come to make a few cuts in the specimen to make sure that the part taken out of the liver contained all the cancerous tissue, that it was surrounded by a generous margin of healthy tissue that had not been invaded by the cancer.

In a few minutes the side door of the room opened and Anna saw, surprisingly in that setting, one of the most beautiful women she had ever seen. She wore a white lab coat over a pale green scrub suit.

'Good morning,' she said to the room in general, smiling. She had naturally red hair, the pale, creamy skin, inclined to freckle, that went with it, and beautiful big hazel eyes under dark arched brows.

'That's Dr Carmel Saigan,' Emma said to Anna quietly. 'One of the pathologists.'

Anna simply raised her eyebrows in surprise that such beauty should be hidden away in the laboratories, which were often located in the basement of a hospital. No doubt this doctor was a very intelligent woman who took her beauty for granted. Anna could just imagine that Dr Saigan had been told from a very early age that she should be in the movies, but not perhaps by those who had had the most influence over her in her impressionable years. Either that, or she had been a very strong-minded individual.

Seth walked over to her. 'Morning, Carmel,' he said, his voice soft. 'Take a good look at this for me, would you?'

'Sure,' she said, smiling up at him as she drew on a pair of rubber gloves.

Anna got the impression that these two doctors had something going between them, although perhaps she was being fanciful, she told herself. These days she was hyper-sensitive to relationships and possible relationships, aware of nuances in the behaviour of others. This came, she thought, from her acute awareness of her own loss. She tended to think that other people were happy, connected, while she was always seeking and not finding, even though her common sense urged her to the contrary at times.

The two doctors stood on opposite sides of the small trolley, their heads close together as they bent over the specimen. They did not touch, as he was sterile and she was not.

They all watched as the pathologist, using her own scalpel, made several parallel cuts into the centre of the specimen where the tumour was located. 'You have good margins,' she said at last. 'This is good.'

Seth turned round to the nurses. 'Emma, Anna, Jay, would you like to take a look at this? It's a classic example of a liver tumour that's confined to one place.'

One by one they looked at the specimen that had been cut open to reveal the tumour. It never failed to leave Anna in awe that these hidden things could be revealed to the human eye. They could clearly see the difference between the tumour of cancerous cells and the healthy tissue that surrounded it, and they all got a sense of satisfaction that they had been a part of solving the problem.

The pathologist took the specimen away with her, and they returned to the job in hand. By the end of the operation Anna was again aware of a very strong sense of professional respect for Seth.

After work she went home on a streetcar, her mind buzzing with all that had happened during the very busy day as she stared unseeingly out of the window while the vehicle clattered along on its tracks. All in all, it had been a good day.

Meeting the beautiful pathologist, seeing her rapport with

Seth, had had the effect on *her*, of making her feel more than ever like the exhausted single mother that she was, trying to juggle the two aspects of her life. Perhaps Dr Carmel Saigan was a single mother, for all she knew. Anyway, beside that woman, with her bright hair and obvious rapport with Seth, she had felt insignificant. Why it should matter, she wasn't sure, but somehow it did.

And she reluctantly had to admit that she did not want to be totally insignificant as far as Seth was concerned. If he were to help her in her search for Simon she would need to have him very much on her side. As things stood now, she could not say exactly what his attitude was towards her. That he was wary of her, albeit in a subtle way, was definite.

When she arrived back in her basement apartment, the first thing she did after taking off her coat was to check her answering-machine. There was one message, and her heart leapt in anticipation as she heard the voice of Hector Smythe.

'Give me a call when you get in, Ms Grey,' he said. 'I'll be in my office until at least six-thirty.' He had left his number, so she dialled it immediately, getting through to him directly.

'I have a little bit of news for you, Ms Grey,' he said. 'We've been able to check with both the Canadian and the United States professional medical colleges, with which all physicians must be registered if they wish to work in those countries, and we discovered that Dr Simon Ruelle is not currently a member of either of them. So we can say with assurance that he is not working in North America.'

'I see,' Anna said quietly, a little more hope dying within her. 'That's interesting information. How did you get it, Mr Smythe?'

'Dr Seth Ruelle got it for us, actually,' Hector Smythe

said. 'We could have got it ourselves, eventually, but he expedited the search for us.'

'Oh,' she said. 'I was working with him today and he didn't mention it.'

'Well, he wants to remain in the background and wants me to be the one to talk to you. After all, it's our investigation. We've been very lucky that he's taken an interest.'

'Yes…'

'He told me he would be in touch again.'

'I see,' Anna said again, a familiar sense of foreboding taking hold of her. 'If Simon isn't working in North America, where could we try next? Assuming he's alive…'

'We're looking for family connections,' he said. 'We have to tread carefully. We have to consider the possibility that he might not want to know that he has a child, and we certainly don't want any other members of his family knowing about it before he knows himself…assuming that he has any other family.'

'Will you try South Africa?' Anna said tentatively.

'That's exactly where we are going to look, at the suggestion of Dr Ruelle,' Hector said, sounding enthusiastic, as though he was really warming to the chase. 'Dr Ruelle has agreed to help us there. We're going to be looking at parts of Africa, as your Simon was born in Zimbabwe, and we're going to look at Cape Town.'

'Why there specifically?'

'The doctor has some evidence that there are Ruelles living there, either not related to him or maybe distantly related, but perhaps more closely related to the missing man.'

'I see. Well…thank you so much.' There was a feeling of sick excitement in the pit of her stomach.

'I'll be in touch, Ms Grey, at least every three or four days, whether we have anything significant to report or not, so that you're not wondering what we're up to.'

'Thank you, Mr Smythe,' she said again.

When she had changed into jeans and a sweatshirt, she went upstairs to see Finn and her mother. Although she was looking forward to a weekend off, she found that she was also looking forward to being at work again. Thank God, she told herself, that the move back to work had turned out to be a positive thing so far. She would keep her mental fingers crossed that it would remain so. Part of her enjoyment was that she liked working with Seth, even though he did not appear to want any direct communication with her about Simon. Maybe that was for the best. At the same time she did not want to examine more closely her enjoyment of his professional company.

'Finn!' she called. 'I'm back!'

'Mummy!'

It was always such a pleasure to hear his voice, to pick him up and hug him, to have his arms around her neck. As she scooped him up, marvelling at how heavy and compact he felt these days, she made a firm attempt to shift her mental processes, to give her full attention to Finn and to forget both Simon and Seth.

'How's my boy?' she said.

'Good,' he said.

The next two weeks went by very quickly. Because Anna was working on Seth's operating days, she saw him and worked closely with him every day she was there. The transition of thinking of him as Seth had worked. When she thought of him, she no longer automatically thought of Simon. This was helped by the fact that they had different personalities, Seth being more serious, thoughtful and quietly wary in a nice way, although he certainly had a sense of humour. Nonetheless, there was a barrier that she felt she had little hope of getting through, and she told herself that it was nothing to do with her.

Often she felt his eyes on her as she went about her work. Sometimes she returned his look, briefly; sometimes she pretended that she was not aware that she was under close scrutiny, whereas in actuality she was acutely aware of him.

Other times it appeared to her that he wanted her to be fully aware that he was assessing her, while giving away little of himself. Much of the time he appeared inscrutable to her. Yet he was unfailingly pleasant, polite and professional.

Inevitably, they met again at the scrub sinks, just the two of them. It was a revelation to her that she could be so drawn to an attractive man. It was very sobering, as well as confusing. Over the years she had carefully nurtured a certain sense of loyalty to Simon, misplaced or not. Whether she loved him was a moot point. Perhaps because of that loyalty, she seldom found men attractive these days. It was partly, too, that she was a tired mother. The fault, if she could call it that, was with her.

So, confronted with Seth, she felt somewhat as though she were going back in time to a period in her life before she had met Simon.

'And how are you, Anna?' he asked, looking at her sideways in that assessing way that unnerved her.

'I'm well, thank you,' she replied, knowing that she was being formal and stiff with him, not knowing how to unbend, even after that light-hearted exchange in the coffee-lounge.

'And I'm really enjoying the work. The liver cases are interesting.'

'I'm glad you find it so,' he said. 'How is the young Finn? I assume he doesn't mind that you work outside the home?'

'He's with his grandmother most of the time,' she said, taking care not to sound defensive. 'They love each other and enjoy each other. I...guess he would prefer that I didn't work.'

'Mmm.'

'I believe that children,' she rushed on, 'need to be with people who love them all the time, until they have a strong sense of self and are able to cope with people who don't love them, or maybe even like them.' She paused, flushing.

'You certainly feel strongly about that,' he said, smiling. 'I agree with you one hundred per cent.'

Anna grinned back, a little sheepishly. It was very nice when he smiled at her—she felt warmed by it. 'Yes, I do feel strongly about it. Hope I don't sound preachy and holier-than-thou. If I didn't have my mother to look after Finn, I don't think I would be working, even if I had to live in poverty. I would have a roof over my head, anyway, courtesy of my parents. Poverty is relative.'

'Why are you really looking for Simon?' he said unexpectedly, as though she had not already explained.

'For Finn. I don't know how I feel about Simon...it's been such a long time. The Simon I knew might not be that person—if he's alive.' For the first time she found that she did not want to hint that she might still have some feelings for Simon, because she didn't know herself how she felt about him now. The image in her mind was of the Simon she had known before Finn's birth. Would she still care for the Simon she would find? If she ever found him...

'Can you still care for someone you haven't seen for years?' he said. 'I know that depends on the circumstances of the separation, but he was not with you during your pregnancy.' Again, he was looking at her astutely as he lathered his hands and arms, while she did the same. 'It wasn't as though he had to go away and fight in a war, or anything like that.'

Anna felt somewhat affronted by the bluntness of his comments, and she was really on the defensive now, even though there was a certain relief in having things out in the open.

'I don't know how to answer that,' she said quietly. 'I know that if I find Simon, he may be a different person. We've both grown up. I know I have, since Finn was born. If nothing else, he'll know that he has a son. Surely that's worth something?' She felt angry and emotional, as though she wanted to cry. It was partly because he spoke sense.

'Yes,' he said quietly, 'it is worth something. I don't want to upset you, Anna, by being curious. It's nothing to do with me really.'

'You're very reticent about yourself, Dr Ruelle,' she said, 'but you expect me to bare my soul.'

'We'll get together some time and I'll tell you all about myself,' he said, smiling. 'Let's be friends, Anna. All right?'

She gave no reply to that, her face flushed as she kept her eyes on the job in hand.

'Friends?' he persisted.

'Yes.'

'Perhaps you'll come out for a drink with me one day, Anna? After work?' he said.

'I… Maybe,' she said.

'I'll take that as a yes,' he said, his tone light.

'Could I, please, have those two photographs back that I lent you, Dr Ruelle?' she asked stiffly.

Finishing the scrub process, she went into the operating room ahead of him. Her conversation with him had left her oddly nervous, fearful that she might be less than competent. So, he had asked her out, even though he had not named a specific day. Did she want that? Yes, the answer came back to her. Yes, she did. It was crazy to feel loyalty to Simon when she didn't know whether he was alive or dead...when he might not feel any such loyalty for her. Yet she did. God help her, she did.

Quickly she began to set up the prep table. A scrub nurse had to be at least one step ahead of the surgeon who was coming along behind her from the scrub sinks, so she had to arrange her set-up in the order that the equipment would be used.

'Take your time, Anna,' Seth said, as she helped him into his gown. 'There's no rush.'

When his eyes met hers, his smiled slightly. Perhaps he did understand after all.

'Thank you,' she said. 'I'll be all right, and I'll be ready.'

'Of course you will,' he said.

As she prepared her set-up, he came over to stand near her. 'With this case I'm going to take out a whole lobe of the liver. He's a lucky man that it hasn't spread beyond one lobe. I did the original gut resection for the colon cancer, then I decided to give him a course of chemotherapy and radiation before taking out the liver tumour.'

Anna nodded. Although it was going to be a long day, as they had a full operating list, it would be an interesting one.

Once the first case was under way, Anna's absorption in her work took over so that she was her usual competent self. Thus, the day seemed to go by very quickly. By the time the transition had been made between the nursing shifts, it was four o'clock.

After changing in the locker room, she said goodbye to Emma and went out into the corridor. As she walked to the nearest stairwell to go down to the ground floor she saw Seth come out through the double doors of the main entrance to the operating suite. Close behind him came the beautiful pathologist, Dr Carmel Saigan.

As Anna hurried towards the stairs, muffled in her warm coat, she pulled her wool hat down over her ears, feeling self-conscious. Unnoticed herself, she saw that the two doctors were totally absorbed in each other, talking and smiling. Then, just before she stepped down the stairs, she saw Seth put an arm around Dr Saigan's shoulders.

Not an envious person usually, she found herself feeling a sense of envy and loneliness that surprised her by its sharp intensity.

It was good to get outside the hospital, to feel the crisp, cold air of early winter on her face. As she hurried to the street-car stop, the cold seemed to bring her back to the reality of her personal situation. Already she had waited a long time for Simon, in suspended animation as it were, so perhaps she should give the search for him a definite time-frame. After that, she would give up the active search. After all, she could not go on paying Hector Smythe, even though he had made an agreement with her that he would only charge her for definite results, not for fruitless searches. Each clue would be worth something to her.

When she gave up the search, would she find another man to love? Someone who would care for Finn like a real father and not just go through the motions? On that score she would never compromise.

CHAPTER SEVEN

AGAIN after arriving home from work, the first thing Anna did was check her answering-machine. Sure enough, there was a message from Hector Smythe. 'Could you phone me this afternoon or tomorrow morning?' he asked cryptically. 'We appear to have got a lead and I prefer not to leave information on your answering-machine. Alternatively, you could come in person. Call me first, anyway.'

Anna sat down, feeling rather tremulous, undecided whether to call him now, as it was getting past office hours. First, she took off her coat, slowly and deliberately and hung it in the cupboard in her tiny hallway, seeing that her hands were shaking. Sometimes when you thought you would be calm about something, you found you were not calm at all, and more often that not you could not control your emotions.

After plugging in her electric kettle in order to make tea, she found the courage to call Hector Smythe's office number. Janet's recorded voice answered, telling her that the office was closed, but to call the emergency number if the matter was urgent.

In a way, she was relieved. This would give her time to psych herself up to receive the news, which she felt must be significant this time. Tomorrow, a day off for her, would be soon enough, she decided.

It was a relief and a pleasure to sit down on her comfortable squashy old sofa that had been donated by her parents, to cradle a mug of tea, put her stockinged feet up on the coffee-table and let her eyes rove slowly around her sitting room that contained cherished objects and pictures that had been hers or her parents' for a long time. As she sipped the tea, she gradually relaxed, withdrawing from the stresses of the day, letting herself give up her persona of operating room nurse and take on the one of being Finn's mother again.

She changed into her usual jeans and sweatshirt, secured her hair in a ponytail with an elastic band. Examining her pale face in a mirror, she saw shadows under her eyes. Working outside the home, even part time, was taking its toll on her physically, yet already she could feel the benefit of the mental stimulation that the work provided, of having the companionship of congenial colleagues. That was something she had missed a lot. Of course, there were inevitably abrasive personalities who could make life difficult, but so far in this job she had struck it lucky.

'Are you there, Anna?' her mother called through the connecting door at the top of the stairs.

'Yes, I'm here.'

'I thought I heard you come in. Would you like a cup of tea? Dad and I are going to have one.'

'Just had one,' she said, 'but I'll have another.'

She could hear Finn running about overhead, and her father's voice talking to him. Tonight she and Finn were having supper with her parents, which was just as well as her energy level was low.

'Mummy! Mummy!' Finn shouted.

'Coming,' she called back.

Later, when Finn had had a bath and was dressed in his pyjamas, seated on the sofa waiting for her to read him a bedtime story, the phone rang. 'Hang on a minute, Finn,' she said, going out into the hallway to answer the call.

'Hello, Anna. This is Seth. I happen to be passing your home and I'd like to drop off your two photographs.'

'Oh…' she said. He was the last person she had expected.

'Is that all right with you? I hope it's not inconvenient.'

'Um…no…no,' she said. 'Where are you?'

'Right outside your house, in my car.' She could tell that he was perturbed by having surprised her, yet she had the intuitive feeling that he was checking her out. He could have given her the photographs at work.

'How did you find out where I live?' she asked.

'I asked Emma.'

'Oh, well, do come in,' she said, flustered, her face flushed and sweaty after giving Finn a bath. 'Come round to the back of the house, along the path at the left-hand side. You'll see a pink door—that's where I am, in the basement.'

She rushed back into the sitting room. 'Finn,' she said to her son, who was ensconced on the sofa, surrounded by books from which he was choosing a story, 'we have a visitor for a few minutes, a man I work with. You just stay there and choose a story. All right?'

'Yes,'

She was at the door, opening it, before Seth had a chance to ring the bell. It was odd to see him there, standing on her doorstep. There was little time to be concerned that she looked untidy and her home very lived-in, with Finn's toys and books strewn about.

'Hello,' he said. He wore a heavy, dark grey overcoat against the cold of the evening, and in his hand he held the envelope that contained the photographs.

Anna shivered in the sudden blast of cold air. 'Will you come in?' she offered. 'Perhaps you would like to meet Finn. He's still up. I have to read him a story.'

'All right,' he said, stepping into the hallway. 'Yes, I'd like to meet him.'

'Let me take your coat. I expect you're in a hurry to get home.'

'I have plenty of time,' he said, handing her the envelope before shrugging out of his overcoat. In the confined space of the hallway he seemed even taller and bigger, making her aware of a certain female fragility as she stood beside him, especially when she felt herself buckle at the knees as she took the weight of his coat.

'This is a very heavy coat,' she said, feeling the remark to be inane, but the first thing to come into her head.

'Here.' He smiled, taking it back from her. 'Where shall I put it?'

'There's a chair in the sitting room.'

Finn was still enthroned among his books when Anna preceded Seth into the sitting room, and Finn looked a little startled to see a strange, large man in his familiar domain.

'Finn,' said, 'this is Dr Ruelle.'

'Hi, Finn,' Seth said, squatting down near the little boy. 'Your mother's told me about you, so I wanted to meet you. I'm Seth.' His voice was gentle and he smiled, not trying to overwhelm the child with a false bonhomie that was so common from adults meeting a child for the first time, which tended to make Anna cringe. 'Your mother and I work together at the hospital.'

Finn, not entirely at ease, stared back, mute.

Anna felt suffused with pride and love at the image of her son, clad in his red pyjamas with the white polar-bear motif on them. His legs stuck out at right angles to his body, his feet were bare and his fair hair was damp from his bath. To her, he looked utterly adorable. Behind Seth's back she swallowed nervously, hovering uncertainly, as she thrust the errant strands of hair behind her ears.

Finn looked straight into Seth's face, with all the honesty and curiosity of the young child. Then he said, 'Are you my daddy?'

Anna caught her breath, her heart giving an extra thud of alarm. Finn had never asked any man that before, and she was torn between acute embarrassment and admiration for his courage at voicing what he was thinking. There was a certain resemblance between Seth and Simon.

'No,' Seth said gently. 'But I think I would like to be. I've always wanted a little kid just like you. I may be related to your daddy.'

Then, to her relief, Finn smiled, although Anna could tell that he was still somewhat intimidated by this big man. 'Um…' she said, 'he isn't usually so…precocious.'

'It's all right.' Seth looked up at her. 'That's part of the charm of little kids, they don't dissimulate. Not like adults, who are capable of telling the most gross lies without batting an eyelid.'

'Yes,' she agreed. 'I like that, too.'

'Are you looking for a story?' Seth enquired politely of Finn.

'Found one,' Finn said, more shyly now, hanging his head and darting quick glances upward.

'What is it?'

'"Lost Lamb".'

'Would you like me to read it to you?' Seth asked, while Anna still hovered, unsure what to do with herself.

'All right,' Finn agreed.

'You must be in a hurry to get home,' she said.

'Trying to get rid of me, Anna?' He looked up at her, his eyebrows raised in amusement.

'No, I'm not,' she said truthfully, holding his gaze. Not for a long time had she felt so oddly shy and lacking in repartee, so gauche. 'It's just that I don't want to impose.'

'You don't impose,' he said softly, not looking away.

'Would you like a cup of coffee or something?' she asked, realising only too well that her social graces had slipped during the past three to four years, when the frequency of playing the role of hostess had gone down to almost zero for her, except with two or three close friends.

'What's the "or something"?' he enquired.

'Well…tea,' she said. 'Or I could run up to my parents' place and get you a whisky and soda.'

'Make it tea,' he said. 'Thank you. And I have to confess that I had those two photographs copied. They could help me if I make a few enquiries. Hope you don't mind.'

'What if I do mind?' she said, wanting to challenge him on something.

'I would give them to you, of course,' he said.

'It's all right,' she said, shrugging. 'I'm grateful for any help.'

She almost ran out to the kitchen, where she had the very

confusing idea that she didn't know where anything was kept and had to open cupboard doors at random. 'Kettle first,' she said to herself, forcing herself to calm down, wondering why she felt so uptight. Perhaps it was because, having protested for so long that she wanted to find Simon, she was attracted to another man.

As she listened to Seth's voice reading the familiar story, she got the tea things ready, and thought how incongruous it was to have him reading to her son.

When she carried the tea on a tray into the sitting room, she saw that Finn had sunk sleepily against a cushion, his eyelids drooping, so she went to his bedroom to get his special blanket and teddy-bear, which were always with him when he slept. When she gave them to him he hugged them to his chest, curled up against the cushion and fell asleep, like the switching off of a light, just as the story came to an end. It was a faculty of children that she envied.

Seth got up and moved to a chair. 'He's a great kid,' he said quietly.

'Yes, he is,' she agreed, warmed by his comment as she self-consciously poured tea into mugs.

'He's a credit to you.'

'Thank you.'

Being able to see this woman in her own home, Seth considered he was getting a more rounded picture of her, with a greater understanding of why she wanted to find Finn's father. Seemingly fragile, she was, in fact, competent and strong in a quiet, assured way, he felt. As she had said, the boy would be asking before too long why his father was not with them. When Finn had said, 'Are you my daddy?' he had been deeply touched, thinking he detected a certain longing in the question.

For her part, as she poured two mugs of tea, Anna was wondering what she would say to him.

'How is your father?' he asked, making it easier for her.

'He got over the operation amazingly well,' she said. 'He's back at work, although not doing as much as he was before. He works at the university, in their chemistry department, in research. This illness will force him to reassess his life. He was a bit of a workaholic before, although he always found time for the family. I hope he won't have a recurrence of the disease. The surgeon said it's unlikely, but it's not easy to live with that fear.'

'No, it isn't easy. Prostate cancer can be fairly innocuous if found early,' he said.

'He appreciates how lucky he is,' she went on. 'He had a routine check-up, when the tumour was found.'

'Good,' he said. 'If only more people would look after themselves in that way. Are you an only child, Anna?'

'No, I'm just the youngest,' she said. 'I have a brother and a sister, both in other parts of the country, in British Columbia. We miss each other very much, especially since Finn was born.'

'Yes, you must,' he agreed.

She dearly wanted to ask him a lot of questions, but instinct told her to be careful, sensing that he was what people liked to call a very private person.

'Do you have siblings?' she ventured.

'Yes. Three brothers and one sister. One brother's in Australia, two in England, and my sister's in the United States. We were all born in Zimbabwe.'

'Do you see them very much?'

'We make a point of getting together quite frequently,' he said. 'We all like to travel, so we take it in turns.'

Anna nodded, trying to picture Seth as a child, with his brothers and sister. In her imagination he looked a lot like Finn.

'I'm the youngest of the boys,' he said. 'My sister's the youngest child. My mother didn't want to give up until she'd got a girl.'

'I was blond, like Finn, when I was very small,' he added.

'Thank you for reading Finn a story,' she said, after which she gulped down the last of her tea.

'It was a pleasure,' he said. 'If you do find Simon—and I expect you will—he should be very happy to have such a son, whatever the circumstances of his life.' He glanced at the photograph of Simon that she had on the mantelpiece.

Anna got the impression that he knew more about Simon than he was telling her, perhaps knew the information that Hector Smythe was going to convey, possibly had even found it himself. 'I don't know, I just don't know,' she said. 'If he were married, he might not be so happy even to know. I agonise over that.'

'Then you will have to be extremely tactful and careful,' he said, looking at her steadily. 'What will you do if he is married?'

'I would still let him know that he has a son—at least, I think I would—then I would back away. There wouldn't be any point in compromising his marriage. I accept that he might not want to have anything to do with me, even if he does want to meet Finn. And if he doesn't want to be a father to Finn in any way, I can at least tell Finn in future years that I found his father and honestly tried to make a relationship for him. I don't mind about myself...I'm sort of coming around to the idea that it really is all over for us. I guess we really were not what you could call a couple, because the time that we knew each other was so short. I know it isn't going to be easy, that's why I'm so glad I have Mr Smythe on my side, to advise me. He's very used to this sort of thing, the epitome of tact, I would say.'

'Mmm. Have you heard from him recently?'

'There was a message today. I have to call him tomorrow. I'm very nervous,' she admitted.

'Getting cold feet?' he asked lightly.

'No, not really,' she said. 'Just scared, because I'm so mixed up about certain things, how I really feel.'

'Sometimes you don't know how you feel until you're confronted with an alternative,' he said.

'Yes. This is something I have to do, this search. Would you like more tea?'

'No, thank you,' he said, standing up. 'That was good. I really must go now, I have a dog waiting for me.'

Anna laughed, taken by surprise. 'A dog! What sort of dog?'

'A Dalmatian, a female,' he said, grinning.

'Oh, I love Dalmatians. We had one when I was a young child and I've been thinking of getting a puppy for Finn when he's a little older. I can't imagine you with a dog.'

'Why not?'

'Well…' she said, blushing, 'you're out working all day, for one thing, and…'

'And what?' he said.

'I can't imagine you…um…caring for a dog,' she said.

'You're wrong there,' he said. 'I think I care for her very well, and I love her very much. I take her for a long walk every evening, weather permitting, and during the day I have a housekeeper who takes good care of her.'

'What's the dog's name?' Anna said, seeing him in a new way. It was endearing for a large, very masculine man to say that he loved his dog. The idea of it gave her a twinge of envy, and she laughed at herself wryly for envying a dog. Those twinges were telling her something about herself.

'Velvet,' he said.

'That's lovely,' she said, knowing that her face was lighting up as she remembered her own dearly loved dog. 'They have such soft, velvety ears.'

'Perhaps you and Finn would like to meet her some time?' he said.

'Oh, we would.'

He was putting on his coat before she fully realised that he had more or less confirmed that he wasn't married—although she had a sense that he had been in the past—and that he had indirectly asked to see her again outside work. That prospect left her unaccountably disturbed and gratified at the same time. Without her having to ask many direct questions, he had, perhaps inadvertently, given her some information about himself. Or perhaps she was reading too much into it and he had simply been making conversation.

Anyway, a man who could love a dog must be all right, she told herself.

At the door she said, 'Thank you for bringing the photographs, and my apologies to the dog for keeping you. Goodnight.'

He laughed. 'Goodnight, Anna.' He placed a warm hand against her cheek, surprising her. It was as though he wanted to touch her and could not help himself. Perhaps he was responding to something that he sensed in her. The unexpected contact sent a shiver of acute awareness through her. It was an intimate gesture, gentle and kind, yet not presumptuous or invasive of her personal integrity, she felt. Involuntarily, she swayed very slightly towards him.

Perhaps taking that as a cue, he bent down and kissed her, his lips warmly on hers, his hand still holding her face, his fingers moving under her chin. Startled, she did not pull away but closed her eyes. Slowly he put his arms around her, holding her firmly against the wool of his coat, while her heart thudded in recognition that this was what she wanted.

Anna allowed herself to rest there, against him, giving herself up to the physical contact that she realised she had wanted from the moment she had set eyes on him. For a long time, it seemed to her, they stood there together, the mutual attraction holding them in an intensity of feeling. Her arms moved up to his shoulders.

He was the one to pull back, looking at her with darkened eyes. 'You're a very sweet girl,' he said softly. 'Something must have happened to Simon, because he would have been mad to leave you.'

'I'm not a girl,' she said, hearing sadness in her voice. 'I feel old a lot of the time…so old and weary.'

'You're beautiful and sweet,' he said, kissing her again.

When they stood apart, they looked at each other and he reached forward and took both her hands. 'I admire you, Anna Grey,' he said. 'You have a lot going for you, and you don't realise it. I admire your strength.'

'Is that me you're describing?' she said, smiling up at him in surprise and stepping back. If she wasn't careful, he would indeed have reason to think that she was a woman who got into an intimate relationship too soon. The vibes between them were as powerful, or more so, than anything she had ever felt with Simon. That in itself was confusing, eliciting a sense of odd mourning, as though she was saying goodbye to that young Simon for the final time.

'Yes, it is.' He stroked a strand of her hair away from her face. 'I'd like to get to know you outside work…away from Simon Ruelle. Just you and me, Anna. Can you put Simon out of your mind for a while? Is that possible?'

'I…I don't know, Seth.' What she lacked with him was confidence. So much she wanted to say yes. Was she equal to what he seemed to be offering her? 'I don't actually think of him all the time. I'm doing this for Finn, I really mean that.'

'You seem to be letting the past dominate your present and keep it static, Anna. I do that, too, of course,' he said, looking down at her seriously. 'So, please, don't take that as a criticism.'

He put a hand on her neck, underneath her hair, and eased her head gently towards him as he bent down to kiss her. 'Say yes,' he murmured, just before his lips found hers again.

'Yes,' she whispered, when he moved back from her. 'I'd like to get to know you, Seth. Nothing to do with Simon.'

'We'll take it from there, then,' he said.

'You know a lot about me, Seth, whereas I don't know much about you, and it leaves me feeling at a disadvantage.'

'I'll tell you before too long,' he said.

He dropped her hands, turned from her and opened the door.

'Goodnight again,' he said. 'See you at work, Anna. You take good care of yourself, and that son of yours.'

'I will. Goodnight.'

Then he was gone, out into the cold night, leaving her with a sense of loneliness so acute that she didn't know how she would bear it. But for the tingling of her skin and lips where he had touched and kissed her, she could almost think for a few moments that she had conjured him up out of her imagination, out of her extreme loneliness and need. So he wanted something with her. The very idea left her gratified and confused with longing. Yet he was an unknown entity to her, apart from the sense of trust that she had where he was concerned, having seen him at work and in his efforts to help her.

Sighing, she went back into the sitting room to lift Finn up very carefully to carry him to his bed. As she went she glanced at the photograph of Simon on the mantle, recalling that Seth had looked at it several times. The remote Simon was being supplanted by the very real Seth, who was filling her consciousness.

As she looked at Simon's attractive, smiling face, with its definite resemblance to Seth, she had a powerful premonition that if she found him alive he would be very changed.

That would be the reason for his silence.

Later, as she was getting ready for bed, the telephone rang again.

'Anna, it's Em.'

'Hello, Em. What's up?'

'Well, Dr Ruelle asked me for your address and I gave it to him, and since then I've been wondering whether I should have given it out. I wouldn't usually do that, it's just because it was him and I trust him. Sorry if I did the wrong thing.'

'It's all right, Em,' Anna said. 'He wanted to return two photographs that he had borrowed from me. He may be able to help me look for Simon.'

'He came round there?'

'Yes.'

'That's all right, then. I wasn't sure what you really thought of him.'

'Well…' Anna said hesitantly, 'off duty he seems like a genuine person—nice, the way he is at work, but nicer, not quite so wary. I was surprised, but I didn't mind. I think he wanted to suss me out, and to meet Finn as well. If he finds out anything about Simon, he isn't going to divulge it unless he knows and trusts me, I'm sure, especially if they're related.'

'No, I can understand that. He seems to be a very careful sort of person,' Emma said thoughtfully. 'Someone told me just the other day that he's been married and divorced, that his wife, who was a doctor, didn't want to have children, and he did. I don't want to gossip, but I know you won't repeat it. I was told by someone who knows his former wife. There must be more to it than that, I think.'

'Yes, I should think so,' Anna said. 'I sort of sensed there was something like that in his background. I'm not sure how I knew. It's sad, because I get the impression that he cares about it a lot. I can't say how I know that. Of course, I couldn't ask…none of my business.'

'People give off certain vibes, I think,' Emma said, 'and we pick them up if we're at all sensitive.'

'Yes. It's strange.'

'I get the impression that he likes you,' Em said.

'I think he's mainly being kind,' replied Anna, believing that, even though he had held her in his arms and kissed her, although he had said he wanted something between them. It had been a response to her loneliness, and perhaps to his. 'And I think he maybe has a relationship with Dr Saigan.'

'Oh, I don't think so,' Emma replied. 'I think they commiserate because she's divorced too and has a small son with cerebral palsy. When she needs someone to talk to, he lends an ear.'

'I'm sorry to hear that. Just shows you really don't know, most of the time, what other people are going through behind an apparently cheerful exterior. Maybe he's doing the same with me, just being kind.'

'Time will tell. Well, goodnight, kid. I must hit the sack.'

'Thanks for calling, Em. See you anon.'

In bed she lay sleepless for some time, thinking about Seth. The gossip may or may not be true. The memory of his kisses was vivid in her mind—they changed everything. Now she was missing him, wanting to see him. Lying there, staring at the ceiling, she could not help wondering if he was missing her.

Some things were falling into place now, as she found that she wanted a relationship with Seth more than she wanted to find Simon. There was guilt in her for that. And what would Seth really think of her if she tried to live more in the present, with him? That was in spite of what he had said.

For once, she was falling asleep not obsessing over Simon…

CHAPTER EIGHT

FINN woke early the next morning, as was his wont, and that of most small children, so Anna had discovered from talking to other mothers. Later, when you wanted them to get up to go to school, the early-bird habit had changed somewhat, so she had been told.

After they'd had breakfast and he was playing on the floor with his toys, Anna called Hector Smythe's office, feeling nervous.

'Ah, Ms Grey!' he said ebulliently, as though he had just been waiting for her call. 'Good to hear from you, and I have some good news. We've discovered, with the help of Seth Ruelle, that your Simon is registered to practise medicine in South Africa.'

'Oh, my God,' she said. 'That means he's alive! I...I saw Dr Ruelle yesterday and he didn't say anything about that.'

'He wants me to impart the news. That's not all. There are some Ruelles living in Cape Town, so we assume that he may be working there. We are in the process of checking that out, as well as checking the family connections.'

'Oh...' She felt a little sick from excitement and a certain apprehension that her hopes were apparently coming to fruition.

'Dr Ruelle seems pretty sure that they are related to his family, although he told me that he doesn't know them personally. He's indicated that he would be willing to be the one to make contact, to make some enquiries about Simon. It's of interest to him personally also, so he told me.'

'I see,' she said, her voice shaking.

'It shouldn't be too difficult,' he continued. 'If he can contact one person who is willing to talk to him, then he can maybe proceed from there. He does not have to divulge initially that he is enquiring for someone else. He can say that he has decided to look up the other branches of his family and that he has been wanting to contact Simon for a long time, as he now works in Gresham, Ontario himself.'

'That sounds reasonable,' she said. 'Thank you so much.'

'Now, you just sit tight,' Hector Smythe said, 'and I'll be in touch in a day or two, with something else very definite, I expect.'

'Yes. Should I...should I say anything to Dr Ruelle when I see him at work? To at least say thank you?' she enquired.

'That's up to you,' he said. 'My feeling is that you should wait until he has contacted an individual in the family in Cape Town, because then he will have to draw you in, I should think, if contact between you and the family is to be made. I think we might need Dr Ruelle as a facilitator there. So perhaps you should keep quiet and wait for that next development.'

'All right,' Anna agreed. 'Do you mean that I might have to go to South Africa?'

'It's possible, but it will be rather tricky from then on in.

It will only be if they want you to. We may find that he's married, with other young children. Don't get your hopes up too high, Ms Grey.'

'Oh, I'm not,' she said, finding that she meant it. 'I just want some answers and for Simon to know about Finn.'

'That's good,' he said.

Talking to Hector Smythe was always good, she reflected, because he had a precise, common-sense way of imparting news that had the effect of forcing her to clarify her thoughts. Surprisingly, as they seemed to be closing in on the real Simon, rather than the one that had lived in her mind for so long, she was becoming more realistic about what he could mean to her. From Simon's point of view, not knowing he had a child, he would have moved on with the passing of time in a way that she had not.

'Well,' he added. 'I'll be in touch.'

'Thank you,' she said.

She walked around the kitchen, not knowing quite what to do with herself. The information still left many questions unanswered. That Simon was registered to practise medicine in South Africa implied that he was capable of working. At least, that appeared to be the case. She must try to keep an open mind and just wait for further information.

She made herself some coffee, automatically going through the motions, then took it into the sitting room to watch Finn playing. Her emotions were all over the place. There was nothing straightforward about this, she sensed. Restlessly, she sipped the coffee, feeling suddenly claustrophobic in the small apartment. Soon she would take Finn out to a park and playground, even though the weather was cold. They would bundle up warmly, then after that she would run a few errands. She needed that fresh air to clear her head. It was a good thing that she had a day off as she felt too agitated to concentrate on anything precise. With Finn she could relax eventually.

Restlessly, she went to the small laundry room where she kept Finn's stroller and pushed it out to the sitting room, then collected warm rugs from a cupboard and his outdoor clothes. She got her own outdoor clothes ready and her boots. When under mental stress, she had found over the years that it was good to go for a brisk walk, especially to commune with nature, so that she could think more clearly, the physical activity somehow defusing the mental turmoil somewhat.

'Come on, Finn,' she said, 'we're going for a walk in the park, then we're going to the shops to buy something for supper.'

'See pets?' he said.

'Yes, we'll go by the pet shop,' she promised. Finn would like to have a kitten, but he was too young to know how to handle one.

It was good to get out in the fresh, crisp air, to walk at a brisk pace, pushing the stroller with Finn in it.

'Duck pond?' he said.

'We'll go by there,' she promised, 'but I think some of the ducks may have flown away for the winter to a warmer place. Then they'll come back when it's warmer, in the spring.'

As Anna walked, the cold air helping to clarify her thoughts, she knew then how frightening it could be to have your desires realised or, put another way, having success in what you'd said you wanted. Maybe that was why some people behaved in such a way as to sabotage themselves—and made that a habitual mode of behaviour. Fate, as well as the consequences of her own efforts, she could say, had called her bluff and now she felt herself with a sense of panic greater than anything she had experienced before. Now the final truth would come out. She would find out eventually what had happened to Simon, and also discover whether he had ever intended to have a permanent relationship with her, marriage or otherwise.

Events were moving along at least partially out of her control. She could withdraw from it all perhaps, but had elicited the help of several people, and if she did not go forward now the remaining mystery of this story in which she found herself would tantalise her for the rest of her life.

Even in this sense of panic she knew there was no alternative but to go forward.

For two hours they walked, first in the park then along a street of shops, where Anna took Finn into a familiar café where she could get good coffee for herself and hot chocolate for him after they had been to the pet shop. Half her mind was on the dilemma of Simon. What if he wanted nothing to do with her, or Finn? Perhaps with Hector Smythe and Seth acting as go-betweens for her, she might never have to confront that issue on her own.

Finn was asleep, swathed in rugs in the stroller, when she pushed him quietly through the pink door of her basement flat. Just as she shut the door, the telephone rang, and she ran to answer it so that it would not wake Finn.

'Hector Smythe again.'

'Oh, hello.'

'I've more news, Ms Grey,' he said. 'Dr Ruelle has been very busy on our behalf. I've just had a lengthy conversation with him, in which he informed me that he's made contact with the family.'

Anna's chest felt suddenly tight. 'Oh…that's amazing.'

'He's actually spoken to someone on the telephone in Cape Town, Simon's sister, Sophie. She seemed willing to talk to Seth, after he had established his credentials and they talked about the extended family. He said, in fact, that she seemed very relieved to be able to unburden herself to him, as apparently she has been responsible for Simon for some time,' Hector Smythe said.

'Responsible?'

'You must prepare yourself to be strong. Simon was indeed involved in an accident. It happened in Boston when he went there to visit his sick mother, all that time ago,' he said.

'Oh… Oh, dear.'

'Seth has suggested to me that he should be the one to tell you the story, as he has all the information from the sister,' Hector Smythe said. 'I think that's a good idea, so that I don't have to repeat it all and maybe forget some of the details. He would like you to call him. I have the number here.'

'Dr Ruelle…did say once that he might not necessarily divulge information to me,' she said. 'It looks as though he's changed his mind.'

'Oh, yes. Now he knows that there definitely has been an accident, it's a different story.' He gave her Seth's telephone number. 'That's his office number and he wants you to call him there as soon as possible.'

'Thank you so much, Mr Smythe,' she said breathlessly. 'After I've spoken to Dr Ruelle, what's the next move for us?'

'Dr Ruelle will tell you. Apparently the family is seriously thinking of emigrating to western Canada.'

'Oh… It's all happening so quickly.'

'Yes, it often is that way, once you get a few definite clues.
You call Dr Ruelle now, Ms Grey, then I'll call you later in
the day so that we can have a chat about how things went and
to plan the next moves.'

'Thank you.'

Carefully she removed her outdoor clothing and got
herself a drink of juice from the fridge before she was able
to summon up the courage to punch in the number of Seth's
office.

'Dr Ruelle's office,' the suave voice of his receptionist
answered, so that Anna had a mental image of the attractive woman.

Quickly she was put through to him.

'Seth, it's Anna Grey. I…I understand that you have some
information for me, that you would like to talk to me in
person.'

'Yes, Anna. Could I come over to see you now?'

'Over here? Well, y-yes,' she stammered. 'Is it…is it bad
news?' Her voice lowered on the final syllables as she felt
herself wanting to cry.

'Yes and no. Simon was indeed in an accident, but he's
able to work, after a fashion. He has all his mental faculties.
I've spoken to his sister.' His voice was gentle. 'I prefer to
tell you face to face…it will be easier for both of us.'

'All right.'

'I'll be there in about fifteen minutes.'

'Thank you…for all you've done.' She hung up quickly,
feeling her throat close up and her eyes fill with tears.

She decided to leave Finn in his stroller, to push it into his bedroom and let him sleep on while she listened to what Seth had to say. Then she brushed her hair and made coffee. A kind of strange calm came over her as she moved about, performing tasks. So Simon had been found. In a way her faith in him had been vindicated, the faith that he would not willingly have disappeared out of her life. A deep thankfulness for that vindication filled her.

On cue, Seth arrived. She watched for his car being parked on the street, then opened the door to wait for him. When he came in, she was immediately struck by how tired he looked, pale and haggard. His presence calmed her. 'Hi.' He smiled at her, shrugging out of his coat. 'How are you taking the news?'

'The relief is tremendous, on the one hand. Then, on the other hand, I'm sort of sick with apprehension about the accident that he's had. Will you have some coffee? I've made some,' she said quickly. 'I'm hoping we can say all there is to say while Finn is asleep. We just went for a long walk. And thank you for coming, for taking time away from your office.'

'I'd appreciate some coffee.' He followed her into the kitchen. 'I've become as obsessed as you are, Anna, to get all this sorted out.'

'I'm sorry…for you,' she said. 'But not sorry for myself that you're doing it. I'm more grateful than I can say.'

Nonetheless, as she moved about her tasks, she was very conscious of a strange and unexpected sense of panic in her that Simon had been found. What was all that about? Her chest and throat felt tight with something like hysteria.

With mugs of coffee in front of them, they sat at the kitchen table.

'I've made contact with a Sophie Ruelle, who is Simon's sister, in Cape Town, through a few old medical contacts I have there,' Seth said, without preamble. 'I told her I wanted to find members of my extended family, and that Simon's former colleagues in Gresham had been wondering where he was…how he was.' He took a swallow of coffee, looking at Anna, who sat on the other side of the small table. He was obviously weighing his words very carefully, and she felt a sense of dread that was very familiar. 'To get right to the point, he's there, living with her.'

Anna swallowed painfully, clasping her hands together, looking fearfully at the man in front of her, the sense of ambivalence and panic increasing. 'Tell me about the accident,' she said, her voice barely audible.

'Yes, I will. First of all, I want to apologise to you for doubting your interpretation of events for a while,' he said, leaning towards her. 'Your intuition served you well.' To her surprise, he reached forward and squeezed her clasped hands for a few seconds, which had the effect of calming her. 'Take it easy.'

Anna nodded, her eyes filling with tears, and she found that she could not look at him as she kept her eyes down, fixed on the mug of coffee in front of her.

'I'll tell you what Sophie told me,' Seth said. 'It's rather like a jig-saw puzzle, with a few bits still missing. As you know, Simon went to Boston to visit his mother, who was in a hospital there. He stayed at a friend's apartment who was out of the country for six months. The friend had told him he could use it at any time, had given him a key. He arrived in Boston late in the evening, too late to see his mother, apparently, as there is no record that he visited the hospital. Early in the morning he got up and went for a run, jogging around several blocks. When out, he was hit by a car while crossing a street. He was taken to hospital, unconscious, where it was found that he had no ID on him. All he had was a door key, with no indication of an address.'

'Oh, poor Simon,' Anna whispered, closing her eyes tightly, as tears squeezed beneath her lids. So many times in her imagination she had seen such a scenario.

'He was unconscious for several days, then when he regained consciousness he could not remember his name or where he lived. While all this was going on his mother died, was cremated and her ashes shipped to South Africa.' Seth's voice went on softly, relentlessly, as though he wanted to articulate all that he knew while the details of the story were sharp in his mind.

Anna was crying openly now, unable to help herself. She put her hands over her face.

'He did eventually remember his name and where he was staying. He also discovered that he was paralysed from the waist down from a spinal injury where the vehicle had hit him. He also had a head injury.'

Seth handed her a handkerchief from his pocket, which she used to cover her eyes.

'He spent quite a while in that hospital. When it was time for him to be discharged, his sister came to get him from South Africa to take him home with her. He was in a wheel-chair and suffering from depression because he thought his career was over, among other things. He had wanted to be a surgeon, as you know…was a surgeon.'

Anna nodded and sobbed into the handkerchief.

'The subsequent severe depression was probably responsible for the fact that he did not contact you, or a lot of other people. He had, fairly early on, contacted his boss in Gresham to let him know that he would not be back. Sophie told me that he was so depressed that they thought he was suicidal and did not leave him alone for many months.'

'Oh, dear…what an awful thing,' Anna whispered despairingly. 'Did he…? Does he…say anything about me?'

'Sophie mentioned that Simon had had a girlfriend, but he refused to have her—you—contacted because he felt he was of no use to anybody, least of all to you. She didn't press the issue, not knowing your name. Had they known you were pregnant, I imagine it would have been a different story.'

Seth stood up, large in the tiny kitchen. 'May I help myself to more coffee?'

Anna nodded, taking some swallows of her own coffee, which had lost a lot of its heat. Seth filled his mug and replenished hers as well. 'It's a sad story,' he said, leaning back against the counter. 'Sophie told me that he's working with a surgeon who does hand surgery, microsurgery on hand trauma cases. It's something he can do sitting down. He can't walk, of course.'

Anna looked up at him with tear-filled eyes. 'Is that it?' she asked.

'Yes, more or less.'

'I'm relieved to know,' she whispered. 'Thank you for telling me…for all that you've done. It's a relief to know, but so sad. Simon had everything to live for. He was so young, so vibrant…intelligent and talented.'

Seth put down his coffee and moved the short space in her direction, putting out both his hands. Automatically she took them and he pulled her to her feet and folded her in his arms.

Numbed by sadness, coupled with a tremendous relief that Simon was alive, she went willingly. With her head against his chest, they stood and waited while she tried to compose herself. It felt so good to be held by him, to be comforted. She felt no self-consciousness, it seemed perfectly natural.

She pressed the ball of his sodden handkerchief against each eye in turn. A stirring of longing began within her, to be wanted and loved, to have someone to share with, even this grief—especially this grief.

'Sorry to be the bearer of such news,' he said softly.

'Rather you than someone else. I have to be honest and say that I'm very mixed up about all this. Now that I know he really is still alive, I feel nervous about going on with it.'

'That's understandable. You'll feel better if you see it through, I think, Anna. In many ways it could have been worse. At least, now you know that he did not willingly desert you, that he's alive,' he said. 'Perhaps now you can begin to see your way forward.'

'Yes, it could have been worse,' she whispered. She found that she did not want to move away from Seth, that she wanted to stay there for a long time. His closeness warmed her in a way that she had forgotten about. His attraction was an added dimension to what she thought of him, eliciting shyness in her yet a fledgling, delicate flowering of something else…a rise in confidence, a struggling sense that she could be loved again, that she was lovable and attractive as a woman.

'You're doing very well,' he said.

'I don't know about that,' she said tremulously.

He kissed her, stroking her hair back away from her face.

'I could become addicted to this,' she said. 'I don't want to move.'

He laughed. 'That's all right. On both counts. Come.' He took her hand, picked up the two mugs of coffee and led her into the sitting room to sit on the sofa, where they sat side by side. He put an arm around her shoulders, pulling her head down to rest against him.

'Let's just be quiet for a while,' he said. 'I have more to tell you, but that can wait.'

This woman, Seth considered, was so different from his ex-wife. There was a quiet strength about her mixed with a vulnerability that was somehow endearing to him. And another big difference was that she was not loath to show her vulnerability. She appeared to think it was the normal thing to do, to confess one's anguish and weaknesses, because that was not all one was.

The other person had to accept you for what you were, or not at all, she seemed to be saying. There was no subterfuge in her, something that he found rather amazing and very refreshing. That was, he thought now in retrospect, one of the things that had attracted him to her from the time he had met her, although he had certainly put up resistance to it.

Now that he held her hand and had an arm around her shoulders, there seemed to be nothing else in the world that he would rather be doing. The fact that she needed him raised in him unexpected emotions of tenderness that were not tinged, for once, with wariness. That much she had done for him.

'Thank you for being here,' she said.

In answer, he squeezed her hand. 'I'm an old-fashioned sort of a guy,' he said, after a while, 'who likes to hold hands.'

'I'm glad you do,' she said softly, her head against his shoulder.

After a while, they drank the remains of their coffee. 'Are you ready to hear more?' Seth asked. 'There's something interesting I have to add.'

'All right.'

'Simon, with his sister, will be coming to Boston soon for a medical check-up at the hospital where he was treated after the accident. He has doctors in South Africa who're looking after him, of course, but he comes back to Boston once in a while for assessment. They haven't written him off,' Seth said.

Anna sat up straight and looked at him. 'I'm glad about that. Does he know anything about me?'

'No. His sister and I agreed that you should be the one to see him, to tell him. Once he's in Boston, she will ask him if he wants to see you. If he does, then you can tell him about Finn.'

Anna nodded. 'Yes.'

'Sophie has agreed to contact me when they know the dates and details of their flights,' Seth said. 'She also asked me if I would like to meet him, as that was ostensibly the reason why I contacted her in the first place. She doesn't know that you had employed a private detective to find him. I told her that Simon has a son, but she has promised not to tell him ahead of time.'

'Would you like to meet him?'

'Yes, I would. We could maybe travel down together, you and I, if you would like to, Anna.'

'That would be good,' she said. 'It's going to be something of an ordeal for me. I don't know how I'm going to react when I actually set eyes on him.'

'Sophie said that he's very changed, so you must try to prepare yourself as best you can. Not an easy thing to do.'

'No…'

'There's something else.' He turned sideways to look at her, assessing her emotions before speaking. 'His sister told me that he has a young woman who wants to marry him. Apparently, the young woman took the initiative in this. She was his nurse when he first went back there, and she's been in the picture ever since. It looks as though it will happen eventually, so she said, but he's reluctant to take on marriage because he's disabled, and it wouldn't be a normal marriage. He's still very depressed about his situation. It's doubtful that he would be able to father a child.'

'I see,' Anna said, sighing. 'I've…more or less come around to the idea that our situation is hopeless. I think I knew, deep down, that something like this had happened and that there was no hope of a future for us. Even so, I know it's going to be strange, letting go of him…as far as I ever had him. I suspect that he's thought of me far less than I've thought of him.'

'That's to be expected,' Seth said gently, 'as you're the one with a child.'

Seth went into the kitchen to refill their coffee mugs, wanting something to do. His attraction to Anna was beginning to disturb him. He found now that he wanted to mean something to her other than just as a passing friend and colleague, whose function would be over when she had settled her emotional connection to a crippled man, had established whether that man was to be in her life in any way as the father of her child.

This was really the last thing he needed in his life, even though he knew that at some point he would want to establish a lasting relationship with a woman. The sheer awfulness of his break-up with his wife, and their marriage towards the end, had left him in a mind set where he constantly drew back if he felt himself to be strongly attracted to a woman, but even more so if they responded to him with enthusiasm. He knew it was obtuse, but he could see where it was coming from.

Time and again he watched himself as though he were a bystander, pushing women away from him when they became too close for comfort. With Anna it was different, as she was at least partially engaged emotionally with another man. Because she was not entirely free in that sense, he was intrigued by her. In another way she represented a challenge, for her very unavailability, which he knew was doubly obtuse.

He added sugar to his coffee and stirred it slowly, stalling for time to think.

Carmel Saigan would marry him, he sensed that, if he were to contemplate marriage again. They had so much in common. She was lovely in every way, yet there was something missing, a chemistry, a spark. He was not attracted to her and could never imagine himself in love with her.

The woman who had become his wife had been determined to marry him, and he had been flattered. She was older, more established, very confident to the point of being abrasive, a respected professional woman, as well as very beautiful. It was not a good idea to marry because you were flattered, he thought wryly as he took a swallow of hot coffee, any more than it was to try to achieve a permanent relationship with someone with whom one's feelings were not entirely reciprocated.

With his wife, when the first flush of sexual attraction had died away, he had discovered that he did not love her. There was something very hard and ruthless about her, concentrating on her career to the exclusion of everything else except her passion for him. Eventually, he had been repelled by it. He had provided the balance. He had found that her passion had not been enough for the two of them.

Compared with his state of mind now, he had been immature then, even at the age of twenty-nine, when they had married. Never would he go blindly into a relationship again.

Now he saw himself getting entangled emotionally with Anna, not only wanting to help her but telling himself that he wanted to discover his long-lost family. How true was that? At least she was not pursuing him avidly, relentlessly, as some women did. She responded sweetly to his kisses, took what he had to give without demanding more. Yes, she was attracted to him, he could see that, but he suspected that she wasn't going to do anything about it.

Some women conveyed the impression that whatever you gave to them of yourself, it was never enough. It was as though they were insatiable and wanted to devour you—your personality, your character, your whole being.

Somehow Anna's sweetness was melting him inside, waking something in him that had been dormant. She seemed to be shrugging her shoulders at him mentally, as though she was thinking, If you've got a queue of women lining up to take you on, don't think I'm going to join it. At that thought, he grinned wryly to himself.

Anna came into the kitchen. 'I thought you'd got lost,' she said, smiling. Her face was pink and blotched from crying.

'Just thinking,' he said.

'Do you want to talk?' she asked quietly. 'Sometimes I get the impression that you would like someone to talk to. What you are doing for me doesn't have to be a one-way street, you know. I'm not just a taker, I know everything is not all about me. I feel happier when I can give something back, fifty-fifty. I can listen and keep a confidence. I don't want to pry into your private life…certainly not that. It's up to you. You've been so kind to me—the least I could do is listen.'

'Some time perhaps,' he said, touched. 'It can wait until your situation has been sorted out.'

'It doesn't have to.'

'I've been married. I'm a pretty mixed-up guy, certainly not in any position to give advice to you. And I don't think I've done that too often, have I?'

Anna found that she could smile now. 'Only to tell me to forget Simon and find another man,' she said.

'Yes, I did say that, didn't I?' he said. 'Rather presumptuous of me. What I would like is for something to happen between us, Anna.'

'A…a sexual relationship?'

'Perhaps,' he said, looking at her astutely. 'But not just that.'

'It's very good of you to want to come with me to Boston,' she said, trying to deflect his attention. 'It will be an ordeal, I know. I thought I'd got some of my emotions under control, but I obviously haven't.'

'We don't always know how we're going to react,' he said. 'We're sometimes taken by surprise.'

'Yes.'

Quite suddenly there was a charged atmosphere between them, as though it had just come out of nowhere. Anna felt as though she could scarcely breathe. There was a tightness in her chest as Seth looked at her intently, as though he could sense everything about her.

'I'm not just being kind,' he said. 'I like being with you, touching you, kissing you. That's even though I wish I didn't. I'm too cynical to be much good to anyone right now. But I can't help wanting…wanting you.'

It would be a lie to say that she wasn't flattered, that she didn't want him, too. 'I didn't want to imply that you were just a kind man, sort of bland and nothing else,' Anna said, struggling for words, tension almost palpable. 'You're a very attractive man, a good man, and I do so much enjoy working with you, being with you like this.'

She swallowed nervously. This sudden change of direction had left her nonplussed, yet strangely relieved as well. Something hidden and secret was coming out into the open. She hated secrets, pretending that things were not as they were. 'As for myself and Simon… Too much time has gone by. I have a sense of loyalty that is misplaced. I know it. It's just for Finn—and then only if I decide that it would be right for him.'

'That's very sensible of you,' he said.

'I don't want you to think that I'm helpless, that I'm taking advantage of the situation to…to get help from you,' she said.

'I don't think that,' he said. 'You gave me a clear choice and I deliberately chose to help. Since I've known you, I've thought of you as a strong person.'

Anna came over to him and put a hand flat against his chest, wanting to touch him. Through the thin black sweater that he wore over a shirt she could feel the warmth of his body and the beating of his heart. 'Seth…'

There were no words for what she wanted to say. She did not know exactly herself what she wanted. They looked at each other, scarcely breathing.

'Anna.' He said her name softly. 'I didn't come here for this, you must believe that.'

'It's all right,' she said, closing her eyes and moving close to him, putting her arms around him, so that it was easy for him to draw her into the circle of his arms.

This time their kiss was different, gentle at first, exploratory, then deeper, as though an initial barrier had been breached. Anna felt herself trembling inside, relaxing against him, giving herself up to the sensations of longing that he was arousing in her.

She put her arms inside his jacket, around his firm chest, his warmth filling her. What it meant she could not think. All that mattered was the moment, knowing that she needed him desperately, on so many levels, as though she had been waiting for him for a long time, holding herself back for him.

She was older now, sober, mature, responsible for another life, unable to concentrate just on herself and what she wanted. Now, in Seth's arms, she acknowledged that she wanted his touch, his manliness, the way he complemented her.

The kiss deepened and they clung together. Time vanished. This moment was all that mattered. There would be time later to ask what it meant, if anything of any significance.

When he pulled back from her, the expression in his eyes was soft, the pupils wide with an awareness of her as an attractive woman. It was a long time since she had seen that expression on the face of a man, and it surprised her in a very pleasant way. She smiled up at him.

'I've been wondering,' he said, 'if you and Finn would like to come to my place for supper this evening. He could meet the dog. She's a friendly dog, good with children, because my housekeeper's grandchildren have been visiting her since she was a pup, so she's used to little kids.'

'That sounds wonderful.'

'I could come back to pick you up later. I have to go back to my office for a while now to see patients.'

'We'd like to come,' she said, moving away from him reluctantly.

'In view of all the news that you've received, I thought maybe you would like a change of scene for a while, rather than being here, brooding about what I've told you. Try to keep an open mind, Anna.'

'Yes…I'll try.'

'I could be here about half past five, or a little earlier. I know that kids have to eat early and go to bed early,' he said, smiling. 'I'll call first, of course.'

'That's good. Thank you, for that…and for coming here in person to break the news. That was much better than hearing it over the phone from Mr Smythe.'

He smiled at her in a way that made her heart feel as though it was turning over. In a way, the intensity of her longing frightened her. Neither of them was entirely free emotionally, it seemed to her, even though they were free in actuality. 'I wanted to come,' he said, reaching for her hand and raising it to his lips. The gesture brought a spurt of tears to her eyes, which she blinked to dispel.

In the hallway he put on his coat. 'Goodbye for now, Anna.'

'Bye,' she whispered, holding the door open for him.

When he had gone, she sat down in the hallway. In a very short time speculation had hardened into facts where Simon was concerned. As she thought about him now, the reality of him was dimmer in her mind. He was moving away from her, to be replaced by the image of Seth…large, masculine, attractive, gentle and very desirable. It seemed amazing to her now that he had held her in his arms and she had responded to the comfort he had offered. It had been spontaneous and natural. Now that Seth was no longer in her apartment, it was as though a light had been switched off. In order to cope with everything, she would take it all a day at a time.

Restlessly, her mind in a turmoil, she went around the apartment tidying up, then washed the coffee things. In her bedroom she got out some clothes that she would wear to Seth's place for supper. He had told her once about the area that he lived in, not far from her, in an old, established area of historical interest.

Finn was still sound asleep, she saw as she crept around his room, getting out the clothes that he would wear later. He looked so adorable sprawled in his stroller, his fine hair wispy on his forehead. She would let him sleep a little longer, then wake him up. In the meantime, she would get on with the never-ending laundry.

CHAPTER NINE

THEY were ready for Seth when he came to pick them up just after five o'clock. Anna had explained carefully to Finn what was happening.

'See dog?' he asked, as he and Anna were settling themselves in the back of Seth's car.

'Yes, we are going to see a dog, a spotted dog,' she said.

The drive to Seth's house took less than ten minutes. It was on a quiet residential street of tall old red-brick houses with attractive small gardens in front, behind ornamental iron fences, and flanked by tall, mature trees.

Inside the house, with its high ceilings and ornate cornices from the 1880s, Anna could see at once that the charming old features of the house had been preserved, rather like her parents' house, which was on a smaller scale, that she loved so much. The atmosphere of the place seemed to draw her in with a warmth that had been established over generations of people who had loved and enjoyed the house. The vibes were good.

Seth strode down a narrow passage that went from the front hall to a door at the back. 'This is the kitchen,' he called back to her. 'I've shut the dog in there. I'll take your coats in a minute.'

In his home he seemed to have undergone a transformation, was relaxed and smiling.

The Dalmatian bounded towards them with a woof when Seth opened the door. She inspected the two strangers quickly, then ran back to her master, her tail wagging furiously. 'Come on, Velvet,' Seth said, patting the dog's head, 'come and meet some friends.'

Anna found herself laughing delightedly at the energy and friendliness of the dog who was sniffing Finn's face and licking him. 'She's adorable,' she said.

Finn, a little apprehensive at first, laughed as the dog licked his face and then his hands.

'Let me take your coats,' Seth said, helping her shrug out of her sheepskin overcoat, his hands on her shoulders. She felt clumsy and slow as she took off her gloves, unwound her scarf and removed her hat.

Finn was on the floor, pulling off his boots, so she bent to help him, feeling her face flush. Having been kissed by Seth, been in his arms, she could not go back to the previous relationship, and now she wondered, with some apprehension, what their working relationship would be like.

Unlike a lot of people who wanted to show off their beautiful houses, Seth did not offer to show her around the house, except to point out the layout of the ground floor to her so that she would feel at home. The dimensions of the rooms were spacious, the furniture antique and beautiful, the drapes of heavy swathed silk in muted earth tones. There were cut flowers and potted plants scattered throughout the ground floor, and there were a lot of books and paintings. The place looked lived-in, very much a home, for all its elegance and charm.

For her part, Anna refrained from gushing about his lovely home or making any personal remarks about it, sensing that he did not expect it and would be embarrassed. After being there for a few minutes, she did notice that there were no family photographs on display, no photographs at all.

She wondered whether this had been the home he had shared with his wife, then thought that it seemed very much his house alone, kept in very good order by an expert house-keeper.

'Some of the food is already prepared,' Seth said, smiling at her, putting a hand on her shoulder, a gesture that was un-calculated and made her feel cherished. That, too, was an un-familiar feeling now, something she had missed, and she found herself melting, as though her heart had been encased in ice and was now responding to his warmth.

The image of him with his arm around the shoulders of Dr Saigan came to her. His warmth and empathy were not just for her, she knew that.

'I thought we would eat fairly soon, if that's all right with you, as it's a working day tomorrow and Finn must be hungry. Perhaps you could help me with a few things, Anna, and lay the table. I'll show you where things are kept, the silver and the china, the wineglasses. As for Finn, I have a pile of borrowed toys for him to play with while we're doing our thing with the dinner, lent to me by Daphne, my housekeeper, who refuses to be called Mrs Willett, even behind her back.'

Anna laughed. 'That was good of her,' she said.

'The toys are on the floor in the family room, next to the kitchen, so we can keep an eye on him, and I expect the dog will keep him company,' he said. 'We'll eat in the dining room. I've even borrowed a plastic seat for Finn to put on top of the chair, also from Daphne, as she told me I would need one. I just do as I'm told when she's around.'

'That's a booster seat,' Anna said.

'I wouldn't know,' he said, 'but I wouldn't mind having to learn.'

While Finn played, Anna set three places at the huge oak table in the impressive dining room, which was painted a dark grey, with shot-silk blue-grey drapes that changed colour as the patterns of light hit them. 'The silver's very heavy,' she remarked to Seth as he came to stand beside her at the table as she handled the cutlery.

'It belonged to my great-grandmother,' he said. 'Yes, it's not good when you're feeling weak. In which case, plastic is better.'

'Is this all right?' she asked a little later, looking over her handiwork of the finished table, with the wineglasses and the white plates with the simple gold rims around the edges, which must have cost a fortune, she thought.

Seth took two tall silver candlesticks from the immense oak sideboard, put them on the table and lit them. 'I don't get to use all this stuff very often,' he said, 'so we may as well have the candles too.'

'Mmm, lovely,' she said appreciatively.

Seth turned to look at her, the yellow candlelight on his face, mysterious in the room that was already darkening as the day moved towards the winter night, even with a side lamp glowing. 'This is a celebration of sorts, for you,' he said. 'An end to at least some of the speculation.'

Standing there, Anna became more fully aware that he was

out of her league. This lovely house, with its many artifacts that had clearly come from Africa long ago, spoke of a wealth that she had not dreamed of.

As she thought of that, she thought also of her earlier assumption, in what now felt like her youth, that she and Simon would one day marry. In her naïvety, coming from a largely egalitarian culture, she had not thought then that he might not want to marry her, but would perhaps have expectations of marrying a young woman from a background similar to his own.

Had Seth invited her here so that she would come to that very conclusion? The thought made her feel slightly sick, whereas a few minutes ago she had felt that something of a burden had been lifted from her.

The trouble was, she was getting more emotionally entangled with Seth than was perhaps good for her. She had better sober up and get real, both where he was concerned and in her dying relationship with Simon. Her somewhat romantic ideas that Simon would welcome and love their son might not be fact when he was confronted with them, himself a semi-invalid and suffering from severe depression. Perhaps where Simon was concerned, any feelings he had had for her might have died a natural death a long time ago.

'That's perfect,' Seth said, standing just behind her. He put a hand on her bare neck, very gently, caressing her skin with his thumb.

As though stung by an electric shock, Anna spun round to face him, breaking the contact.

'You have a very delectable neck, Anna,' he said very quietly, smiling.

'So I've been told,' she said, surprised at how cool she

sounded when she was really in turmoil, deciding to resist his charm, if she could, until she understood him better, if indeed that was going to happen. Once a man has kissed you, you can't go back to an earlier mode of behaviour, but you can draw back.

'You didn't let it go to your head, though, did you?' he said.

'No. I've been told that I have cute ears, nice ankles, lovely eyebrows…the usual stuff,' she said lightly.

'So you do. You're pretty nice altogether, Anna Grey,' he said.

'Back to business,' she said. 'What about this table? Would you rather be twelve feet away from me or is this all right—close, but at right angles?'

'Give me close any time, even if I have to turn to look at you.'

She gave a few unnecessary tweaks to the objects on the table 'We'll bring the food in,' he said. 'Finn can choose what he wants.'

His housekeeper had put the food, a good variety, in serving dishes, some hot, which Seth had warmed up, some cold, which they carried into the dining room. Anna wished that she was not so intensely aware of Seth, of his every move, his presence near her. He was looking very attractive in an understated way, wearing a simple black turtle-neck cashmere sweater and dark grey trousers, so that she found that she was having trouble keeping her eyes off him.

It was odd that now Simon was within reach, she found that he was, in her mind and emotions, moving further away from her. Perhaps it had been sufficient for her to know that he was alive. For this evening she felt that she wanted to put him out of her mind altogether, because she had been thinking about him too much over the fast few years, so that almost everything else had been squeezed out. There was a refrain in her head now, the voice was Seth's. 'You and me, you and me.' If only it could happen. There was an air of unreality about everything, a blurring of the real and the mythical. Somehow, in her mind, Seth was real.

Tuning into her mood, Seth put a hand on her shoulder before they brought the last dishes from the kitchen. 'Try to put everything I told you earlier out of your mind, Anna,' he suggested. 'Just for now. I know you have an awful lot to think about. Worrying is not going to change anything. Let what will be, be.'

Anna nodded. 'I'm trying,' she said.

Seth put on some light background music, then the three of them sat down. Finn was next to her, high up in the booster seat, so that she could easily put food on his plate.

'Tell us what you would like, Finn,' Seth said. Then he proceeded to explain to Finn what was in the dishes, so that he could understand. There was a soufflé, which Seth explained was made of eggs, quiche and various vegetables, as well as some French fries especially for Finn that Seth had fried himself.

'Eggs,' Finn said, pointing to the soufflé. 'And…um…'

'French fries?' Seth prompted, so that Anna laughed.

'Yes…please. Beans…and…um…'

'Quiche?' Seth said.

'Yes.'

'That should be enough for now,' Anna said, as both she and Seth put food on Finn's plate. 'You can add more later, if you're still hungry.' The scene was so gratifying to her that she had to suppress a rather idiotic urge to grin constantly.

'Orange juice, Finn?' Seth asked, picking up a jug.

'Yes…please.'

'Will you have some wine, Anna? I'm just having mineral water, as I'll need all my wits about me to drive you back home.'

'I thought you were going to say that you need your wits to deal with us.' She laughed.

'That, too.'

'I will have a little wine, please.'

Once they had helped themselves to food, Seth talked to them, drawing them both out about their lives in a very skilled way, while telling them something about his boyhood in Africa, going away to boarding school, then going home for the holidays. He told her about going to school in England, and then living in the United States with his parents. For Finn, he talked about the wild animals that he had seen as a child, and pointed out animals in some of the pictures and masks that he had on the walls of the dining room, as well as soapstone sculptures. Finn looked around him in surprise and fascination.

Very gradually, Anna relaxed. She marvelled at how good Seth was with Finn, who chattered and laughed once his initial shyness had been overcome. The food was delicious. She had helped herself to quiche and asparagus. Seth had opened chilled white wine for her, which was having a soothing effect. They both became less wary underneath the surface banter.

I'm going to enjoy this, Anna told herself. Let tomorrow take care of itself.

For her part, she told him about summer jobs she'd had in Europe and South America, how she had backpacked through Europe with two friends. 'That was in my youth,' she added.

He grinned at her and squeezed her hand, while Finn looked on in silent surprise. 'You're still very young,' Seth said. 'Young and beautiful.'

'Are you flirting with me again?' she queried lightly.

'Perhaps I am flirting,' he said. 'You should get back into the habit of it, Anna. It's an art. I'm rusty myself, though you make it easy for me.'

'Without even trying,' she said lightly.

After a while the scene took on a magical quality for her, and she felt her eyes glowing, as well as her cheeks. The candlelight danced around the room, reflected on the crystal wineglasses and on the silver, on the polished wood of the table.

'Oh, it's snowing,' she said, looking through a window that faced a side garden. The softly falling snow, large feathery flakes, was the final touch to the scene, making them feel cosy and enclosed in warmth. 'Look, Finn, snow!' she pointed out.

Seth got up and put a match to the fire in the room, which had already been prepared with paper, kindling and a few small logs. The flames added to the almost surreal charm of the magnificent room. Finn seemed mesmerised by the flames, the candles and the snow. 'Snow!' he repeated, pointing to the window.

'I think he'll remember this dinner,' she said to Seth, 'for the rest of his life. You know those vignettes that lodge in the mind when we're very young, and stay there for ever? Snow and fire together…and the dog, of course.'

'Yes.'

When they had finished the main course, he put a hand on her arm. 'Stay here,' he said. 'Keep an eye on Finn. I'll clear up and bring in the pudding.'

When he had left the room with their used plates, she gave

a contented sigh and let her gaze wander around. Earlier she had feared that when she was back home she would not be able to sleep when the time came, and would possibly have bad dreams about what Seth had told her of Simon. Already she had had visions of Simon being hit by a car. But now, sitting there, she knew that this scene would be in her mind as she lay in bed, waiting for sleep to come. This lovely room, Finn sitting close beside her on one side and Seth on the other, was etching itself into her mind. The scene was made spectacular by the glow of the fire, reflected in mirrors and in the glass of pictures, on the glossy walls.

How she would love to live in this house, would feel safe and secure here. It seemed solid and enduring, a place that would enclose one with its history, which she felt sure was one of contentment.

Velvet came into the room and stretched herself out in front of the fire on a rug. She added to the elegance of the white marble fireplace surround and mantle.

'There's dog,' Finn said. 'Velvet.'

'Yes, she loves the fire.'

There was a large raspberry and strawberry flan, set in a custard, for pudding, and two bowls containing scoops of ice cream, one of chocolate and the other of vanilla. 'This is soya ice cream,' Seth said, wielding a knife to cut the flan. 'I've made some decaffeinated coffee, Anna. Would you like some? And maybe a small glass of a liqueur?'

'Yes, that would be wonderful. This is the best meal I've had for a long time, Seth. Thank you. And judging by the amount that Finn's eaten, he's appreciated it, too.'

'It's my pleasure. I appreciate your company, more than I can say—both of you,' he said.

For some reason his words made her want to cry, and she bit her lip and blinked rapidly. Over the last few hours she had been so focussed on herself and how she was feeling that she had not thought that Seth might be lonely. He seemed to have so much to offer, to be so sought after, particularly by attractive, accomplished women, that she had not thought he might be like someone who was surrounded by water but not have a drop to drink, so to speak, like a sailor drifting at sea.

Not that she thought she was for him…

She would not presume.

'Did you…?' She hesitated. 'Did you live here with your wife, Seth?' The question had been nagging at her, and now, with the aid of the wine, perhaps, she had the courage to ask it.

'No, this was not our home. We lived in the States for a lot of the time. We were married for about two years.'

'So no ghosts of former wives looking over our shoulders,' she said, relieved.

'No. This house belonged to a university professor and his large family, who had it for decades. It was a happy and busy household, so I heard.'

'Tired, Mummy,' Finn said, after eating his ice cream. He yawned, looking adorable with chocolate plastered around his mouth.

'Could he lie down on a sofa?' Anna asked Seth, wiping Finn's face with her handkerchief. 'Perhaps he'll sleep while we have coffee. I suppose I ought to go soon. Although I don't want to go…it's been so delightful.'

Seth lifted Finn out of the seat and carried him into the front sitting room that faced the street and put him down on a wide sofa, covering him with a rug. It felt strange to Anna to see him carrying her son, an unusual feeling of at last having someone to share the love and the chores, the responsibility of a child, if only as a momentary illusion.

Although her parents helped her tremendously, that was not the same as having a partner. So many times she felt alone.

Anna stroked the hair away from Finn's face. 'Go to sleep for a while, darling. Then we'll go home again in the car soon.' She stayed with him for the minute or so that it took him to fall asleep.

They could linger now over coffee. At the table, she felt intensely sensitised to Seth's presence so near to her. Although the wine had relaxed her, it had also weakened her resolve to keep her distance from him emotionally until she felt more stable. 'I'm so used to speaking in baby language to Finn,' she said, 'that I often wonder if I'll ever be capable of having a proper mature conversation again.'

'You can talk baby language to me any time,' he said, so that she looked at him, her mouth stretching into a smile that she knew was seductive. She could not help herself.

Responding, he took her hand, which was lying on the table near him, and with a finger he traced her lifeline, from the bottom of her index finger down to her wrist. 'You have a long life,' he said softly, looking into her eyes.

'That's what an old gypsy told me,' she said, 'when I last went to a summer fair. I don't suppose she was a real gypsy, but I believed everything she said.'

They smiled at each other, heads close together as they both looked at the palm of her hand. 'You will achieve happiness,' he said, 'with a dark stranger.' When Anna laughed out loud, he went on, 'Of course, he will no longer be a stranger when happiness creeps up on you.'

'Oh? I also know something about palmistry.' She took his hand and studied the lines on it. 'You too will achieve happiness after a turbulent time, and you will have…let me see…six children. Or is it seven? A lot, anyway.'

A certain stillness came over him, so that Anna was acutely aware that she had, inadvertently, hit a nerve with him. Then she remembered what Emma had told her, about Seth having wanted children and his wife had not. At the time she had more or less dismissed that as unsubstantiated gossip, having had her mind on other things.

'Really?' he said. Then he lifted her hand to his lips and kissed the palm, folding her fingers over the kiss. 'As my nanny in Africa used to say, "Keep that kiss in your hand, hold it tight, until we meet again."'

Their eyes met, and she felt hers prickling with tears. 'That's very sweet,' she whispered. 'Did that help you to bear the parting? When you were going off to boarding school in another country, trying to be brave?'

'Yes, it did,' he said softly. He reached forward and lifted her chin up. 'Hey, don't cry.'

'I'm not.'

'Yes, you are.'

He kissed her then, leaning the short distance between them, and she closed her eyes. Then abruptly she got up from the table and went over to the fire, standing to look into the flames.

'I must go,' she said.

'Of course you must,' he agreed.

Above the white marble mantelpiece was a very large gilt-framed mirror in which she could see almost all of the room behind her. As she watched, Seth got up from the table and came over to her, putting his arms around her shoulders as he stood behind her. As they remained like that, his eyes met hers in the mirror in the flickering firelight and the dimness of candlelight.

'Behold, a dark stranger,' he murmured in her ear.

Slowly she turned round within his arms and put her arms around his neck.

'I'd like to pick you up and carry you upstairs to my bed,' he said.

'You'd better wait until I'm willing to walk,' she said. 'If.'

He laughed down at her. 'You're good for me, Anna Grey,' he said. 'You have a way of pricking any bubbles of arrogance that I might have floating over my head. I always think of them as balloons that can be pricked when I observe them in other people...mostly my colleagues.'

'As surgeons go, you're pretty good in that regard,' she said.

'I hoped that by bringing you here I'd make you forget Simon for a while.'

'Oh, I did,' she protested. 'Really. I'm just so sort of emotionally labile. Tonight I'll think of this place, the firelight...' She stood up on tiptoe and kissed him.

It was a signal for him to pick her up in his arms and carry her over to a big, squashy armchair. 'I've been wanting to do this Rhett Butler thing all evening,' he said huskily, putting on an act, so that she laughed. 'Only I thought that Finn might be alarmed.'

'He would be.'

When he sat down with her on his lap, her head against his shoulder, she closed her eyes again when he kissed her, blotting out everything else.

Later, she knew that she must ask him about himself, those questions that were uppermost in her mind, and like a barrier between them, building tension. Very soon she really had to leave. 'Tell me about your past, Seth. I would like to know about your wife…about why you divorced. I want to understand you. If you don't mind, that is…'

'My wife didn't want children,' he said, staring beyond her into the fire. 'Before we were married, she said she did want them. After about six months she confessed to me that she'd had a tubal ligation about two years before, as she'd decided she wanted to concentrate on her career and didn't ever want children. She had lied to me in a very blatant way. Perhaps she thought I would just accept it once we were married…but I didn't. It was the betrayal of trust, not the thing itself so much, although that, too.'

'Oh, Seth,' she whispered. 'What an awful thing.'

'From that moment on I couldn't trust a thing she said,' he went on, his voice flat. 'Our relationship was dead for me. There was nothing left to say. I realised I didn't love her, had never loved her. All I wanted was to get out, as quickly as possible.'

This time she squeezed his hand, then held it against her cheek, as though she could will him by the contact to be comforted. 'I had no idea, of course,' she said quietly.

'That's my story, in a nutshell,' he said. 'I have trouble trusting women—anyone, really. I'm always looking for hidden motives, the real story behind the apparent one. You could say I'm pretty messed up. I can't stand lies. It isn't that I wanted a brood mare. Do you understand, Anna?'

'Yes, I think I do,' she said, clasping his hand in both of hers. 'It was a despicable thing to do. It's…an alien world to me…such machinations. I can't understand it. There must be plenty of men around who don't want children, so why marry one who does?'

'The last thing I want is to feel sorry for myself, or to have anyone feel sorry for me. It was an immense relief to get out, and once I'd made up my mind, it was easy. I didn't look back. I'm telling you this, Anna, in case I seem inexplicable to you. I'm screwed up, you might say. I find that I can't just let it roll off me. One day maybe I'll be able to.'

She nodded.

'She—my ex-wife Belinda, could possibly have had the operation reversed because, as you know, most such operations are done with metal and silicone clips which can sometimes be removed,' he went on, no inflection in his voice. 'But she didn't want to. You see…she didn't want to.'

There was silence for a while. Then she said, 'You did the only thing you could do. What you did was right for you. I mean, it was the honest thing to do. Perhaps it was just as well that she didn't want to…if you didn't love her. Sooner or later, child or no child, you would have known that, and it would have been impossible to live with. One day, you *will* be able to put it behind you.'

'Have you ever been with a person and found that you have absolutely nothing left to say to them? It usually comes out of a betrayal of trust, a misrepresentation of some sort, perhaps cruelty. It isn't a conscious decision not to speak to them. It's that there is nothing more that you can possibly say to them,' he went on. 'It's all so totally finished.'

'Yes,' she said. 'I know it.'

'I hope that hasn't spoiled the evening. Now I've said it, I'm glad I have.'

'I'm glad, too,' she said. 'It helps me to know you…and I want that, Seth.'

I love you…I love you so much. The words spoke themselves in her head, as though she had spoken them aloud, and the apparent certainty of it frightened her. She didn't know where it was coming from, as though from another aspect of herself. She was in danger of becoming very mixed up herself. Now that the evening was almost at an end, she found that she did not want it to end. Although she would be seeing him tomorrow, working with him, that seemed like a long time in the future.

'I'd like to make love to you,' he said softly. 'But I'm not going to until Simon is no longer haunting you—assuming, of course, that you want me. I can be arrogant, I know…'

Because she felt that he was waiting for an answer, that she had to give one, she said hesitantly, 'I do want you. As you say, the time is not right…'

They lay together quietly for long moments, absorbing that information, basking in the intense emotion, thinking of the implications. The tension of attraction between them seemed to hold them together in a circle of warmth. Neither one of them was ready for anything else. Yet there was a promise that was almost a tangible thing.

Anna was the first to get up, reluctantly. 'I'd better take Finn home,' she said.

Seth got up and put his arms round her. 'The next thing that will happen where Simon is concerned,' he said, 'is that I'll hear from Sophie about when they'll come to Boston. It's likely to be in January, she said. Just before they're due to come, she'll tell Simon about you, that you want to see him, but she won't say anything about Finn. As I said before, I think that will be up to you, as you assess the situation.'

'Mmm.' Anna nodded. 'I've waited for this for so long, imagined what it would be like. Now it's going to happen, I'm apprehensive.'

'That's natural.'

They carried the dishes out to the kitchen where they would be dealt with by Daphne in the morning. Then when they had their outdoor things on, Seth carried Finn out to the car, put him to lie flat in the back seat and put a seat belt around him, all without waking him up. There was a smattering of snow on the ground, on the trees and shrubs.

At her house, he carried the sleeping child inside to his bed.

'Goodnight, Anna,' he said softly. 'It's been a pleasure. I wish I could stay with you, but I know I can't. See you in the morning, bright and early.'

'Goodnight, Seth, and thank you again.'

He kissed her on the cheek as they stood at the door, then on the mouth. 'Take care, sweetheart. Don't agonise too much.'

Then he was gone, striding away from her around the side of the house, leaving another set of footprints in the snow.

As she closed the door she thought that she would have no reason to see him outside work now in the business connected with Simon. They would be together when they made the trip down to Boston…if he did not change his mind about going with her. After that trip, any contact that she had with Seth would be about them, her and Seth…if there was going to be anything.

Perhaps he would follow through with the invitation to take her out for a drink. He wanted to make love to her, that was clear, but did he actually love her? That was a question that would be going over and over in her mind. They would both tread carefully now because of what had happened to them in the past, out of their own choices.

Later, as she lay in bed, there was an increasing sense of panic when she thought of Simon.

CHAPTER TEN

DURING her lunch-break the next day, Anna telephoned Hector Smythe from a public pay phone outside the operating suite.

'I have all the information, as far as it goes,' she said to him. 'Dr Ruelle has offered to come with me to Boston to meet Simon and his sister. We don't have a date yet. It's likely to be in January.'

'Good,' he said. 'Before you go, I'd like to see you in my office to go over some possible rights that you might have, if you want to claim any support from Simon. I would prefer to see you face to face, as is my policy. He would have the right to a DNA test, of course, to prove or disprove paternity.'

That scenario was suddenly distasteful to her. 'I'm not sure that I want to go through with that,' she said. Now that she was working and earning a reasonable salary, the money issue was becoming less prominent.

'It will be up to you,' Hector Smythe said, with his usual equanimity. 'But we should talk about legal implications, even if the need for them never arises. You can't really make up your mind until you have seen him and talked to him. Also, your situation could change in the future with regard to money, and you may need something for your son's education, if you decide to go the private route. Then there is higher education.'

'You're right,' she said, 'although it's difficult to think that far ahead.'

'I know it is,' he agreed. 'But you must think that far ahead in this regard.'

'I think that marriage is out of the question,' she said. 'Simon has another woman who wants to marry him, and I assume he wants her. Also, it isn't what I want...even assuming it was an option. And it's not because he's an invalid.'

'This has been a learning experience for you, I can tell, Ms Grey,' he said tactfully, a smile in his voice. 'Call me again when you can come to talk. Give me about a week's notice.'

'I will,' she said. 'Thank you.'

In the operating room coffee-lounge she poured herself a cup of coffee from the urn that was always on the go there, glancing at the large wall clock as she did so. One thing she had had to re-learn about the operating rooms, she thought ruefully, was that you had to watch the clock all the time, as the schedule was tight. She had about five minutes left of her lunch-break in which to down the coffee and relax a little. Some things were falling into place, and that was a relief. Yet at the same time she felt tremulous and sad, in mourning for Simon, not for herself in relation to him.

Seth came into the coffee-room, with two of his senior colleagues. As he walked past her, where she was standing drinking her coffee, he gave her a surreptitious wink. The unexpected gesture made her smile, then she turned away quickly to look out of a window as she felt her face flushing.

They had been working together that morning as usual, and now she was to scrub with him for an abdominal-perineal re-section, a long operation which would probably take them the remainder of her shift. It was usually done for cancer of the rectum.

After quickly drinking the remainder of her coffee, she hurried back to her unit, where she planned to help Emma open up the sterile packs, then get scrubbed well before Seth appeared ready for action.

All morning Anna had felt oddly bemused, with a certain dissonance in her mind when she tried to reconcile the Seth she had come to know over the past few days, outside work, with the more formal one in the operating rooms. His off-duty confidences about his wife not wanting children, and the lies she had told about it, were preying on her mind. It was all right not to want children, of course, but to lie about it was not all right.

'Hi,' Emma said, coming in to room one from the attached clean prep room, just as Anna had opened a gown pack and was putting latex gloves on it. 'Do you reckon we'll finish this case before three-thirty?'

'I wouldn't count on it,' Anna said, starting on opening up the main packs for the case.

'Neither would I.'

For this case they needed two main tables of instruments, plus the bowl stands and other equipment. By the time Seth came into the room, with another experienced surgeon, who was to be his assistant, and the surgical resident and the intern, Anna was more or less ready. She and Em had just finished counting the sponges, instruments and suture needles.

'Are you all psyched up for this, Anna?' Seth asked, as she helped him into a sterile gown.

'Pretty well,' she said.

'That's my girl,' he said quietly, while the others were energetically drying their hands on sterile towels.

Emma was hurrying around like a flea in a fit, as she would have put it, trying to do the usual three things at once or, rather, going quickly from one to the other.

'You're doing a great job, Em,' Seth said to her, taking in her flushed face and her slightly frenetic air. 'I'll do what I can to get this finished by half-past three.'

'No problem,' Emma said. 'I can stay a little late.'

Hearing her, Anna wondered if she would be required to stay late. Having her mother look after Finn was an added bonus, although she did not take her for granted.

The other three surgeons were gowned and gloved, the patient was under the anaesthetic and Seth began the skin prep. There was more or less concentrated silence from then on as each person focussed on his or her job, while trying to keep a handle on the whole picture. The patient was prepped and draped, the instrument tables in position.

'Can I go ahead, Ray?' Seth said to the anaesthetist.

'Sure.'

'Knife.'

Anna handed up the scalpel for the skin incision. It was going to be a long afternoon, during which she could not let her concentration drop for one minute.

As it happened, it was almost half past four when they got out of the room, after their patient had been wheeled to the recovery room just down the main corridor of the operating suite. The evening shift nurses had been busy with other cases, so had not been able to relieve them until then.

'Leave it all to us, girls,' one of them said to Anna and Emma as she came into the room that was now a bit of a mess, with overflowing laundry bins and bowls of dirty instruments, and piles of bloodstained sponges that they had counted off in fives.

'Thanks,' Emma said, pulling off her face mask. 'Come on, Anna, let's hightail it to the lounge to see if there's any tea. I'm going to pass out if I don't get something inside me.'

It was a relief to divest herself of the disposable cap, mask and soiled gown. After washing their hands thoroughly at the scrub sinks, they went to the lounge. As luck would have it, someone had already plugged in the electric kettle so Anna began to rummage through the cupboard for tea bags. 'Do you fancy lemon tea?' she asked.

'Sure. Anything hot and wet.'

'Sit down, Em. I'll make it. I've found some biscuits that look reasonably fresh.'

'Great.' Em sat with her feet up on a small table, her head thrown back against the chair, her eyes closed. 'This is heaven.'

'My feet hurt so much,' Anna said, 'that all I can think about is plunging them into a bowl of icy water.'

Before they had finished the tea, the surgeons who had been working on the case came in, Seth with them. The other senior surgeon spoke to the two nurses. 'Would you both like to join us for a quick drink at the pub over the road?' he asked. 'You did a great job in there. It's my treat.'

'Well, in that case…' Emma said, looking at Anna, 'How about it?'

'Well…' she said, thinking of Finn waiting for her. Emma obviously wanted to go.

'Come on, Anna,' Seth said. 'Just for ten minutes. I'll drive you home, if my pager doesn't go off before then.'

'All right,' she said, standing up. 'We'll get changed and meet you over there.'

'What's with you and him these days, if anything?' Emma said as they hurried down the outside corridor to the nurses' change room.

'Nothing much, apart from the fact that he's helping me look for Simon,' Anna said, trying to ignore the ache in her heart because of her attraction to Seth, and the uncertainty.

'Would you like there to be something? I sense vibes. I told you he liked you.'

'You're very sensitive all round, Em.' Anna laughed. 'Yes, I would like there to be something, but I don't think it's going to happen. He's just a nice guy who doesn't want to get entangled with a woman at the moment. I don't suppose he leads a celibate life and I don't suppose he would mind adding me to the list.'

'Did he tell you that?'

'More or less. But, please, don't spread it around, Em.'

'As if I would! I don't suppose he's promiscuous, he's too sensible for that, and he works a lot, from necessity, so I don't think he's got time for a great love life. He's a full-blooded male, that's for sure.'

'Maybe you're right. But he's out of my sphere, Em.'

Their remarks came to an end as they entered the change room and found several others there, who had worked late. There was a general air of exhaustion about them, with chatter at a minimum, as everyone was anxious to get home. Someone was in the shower that was off the change area.

On her cellphone, which she kept in her locker, she called her mother to apologise for being late, saying that she would be leaving soon. If Seth did indeed drive her home, she would not be particularly late.

'Do you often go out for drinks with the surgeons?' Anna asked as they were leaving the main entrance of the hospital to cross the road to a small side street and the pub, called The Stalled Ox, which was modelled after a typical English pub with a homely, well-used atmosphere.

'No, almost never. They don't often go themselves. This place is full of pagers going off and doctors dashing in and out. I think they feel good because the case went so well today.'

The doctors were already there when they walked into the crowded pub, to find that two seats had been saved for them at a small round table.

Anna ordered a glass of soda water with a dash of whisky. When it came, she was tempted to drink it down in one go, as she was thirsty after the gruelling case, but forced herself to sip it.

Seth, on the other side of the table, looked at her, but she avoided his gaze, knowing that she was sensitised to his presence and might give herself away to their mutual colleagues. Any liaisons between staff members were usually kept very quiet, as no one wanted to tune into the passions of others in the work place.

Anna told herself that Seth's regular attentions simply came out of his kindness and empathy in her situation, the help he was giving her and the fact that he wanted to have a sexual relationship with her. Beyond those things she should not read anything very personal into them or risk making a fool of herself.

'Ready to go?' Seth asked, as soon as she had finished her drink. 'I'll take you too, Em.'

'Thanks,' Emma said, standing up. She lived not far from Anna, in the same general direction.

Emma was dropped off first, then in no time they were in front of Anna's house, at which point Seth's pager went off.

'Wait, Anna,' he said, putting a hand on her arm. 'I'll be having a pre-Christmas party soon for the junior members of my department and some of the nurses. Will you come?'

'I'd like to,' she said. As he called a number on his cellphone, she got out of the car. 'Thank you for the ride.'

'Goodnight.'

As she let herself into her apartment, she experienced a peculiar sense of loss, even though she told herself that she had not had anything much with him, really, so was not justified in feeling loss. Yet she did, a sense of what might have been. She felt Seth was holding back with her until the issue of Simon had been resolved. She would go to his party, where she would be one of the crowd.

As it turned out, Seth gave three Christmas parties at his home, to which she was invited, where he danced with her and talked to her. It felt odd to be in that beautiful house again as one of a crowd, and as she walked around the rooms, looking at pictures and objects that were familiar to her, she longed for that previous intimacy. Perhaps only she had thought of it as intimate.

As he held her there were vibes between them that could not be denied. But, then, he danced with every woman in the place, being the gallant host. Now the search for Simon was over, there was a subtle change that she could not define.

'How will you spend the holiday, Seth?'

'My sister and her man are coming to spend Christmas with me,' he said. 'I'll miss you, Anna.'

At the last party, a week before Christmas, he gave her a parcel for Finn. 'Not to be opened until Christmas Day,' he said, having handed it to her unobtrusively as she was leaving. 'There's something in there for you as well.'

'Thank you,' she said.

More than anything, she wanted him to kiss her under the bunch of mistletoe that was hanging in the hallway in a prominent position. But he didn't.

Christmas came and went, with the usual flurry of activity and enjoyment, with a certain amount of stress thrown in, as always. It was good to be with her parents and her son, to hear from her brother and sister, who planned to visit later on in the year. Old friends of hers, and of her parents, dropped round to the house on Boxing Day, when she had a day off.

The present for Finn, from Seth, was a set of brightly coloured building blocks of various shapes, which he liked. Inside the parcel was a present for her, a necklace made of silver and deep blue beads, very lovely.

Looking at herself in the mirror in the privacy of her bedroom, with the necklace resting against her neck, she knew that she would treasure it always. She longed to see Seth over the holiday, but did not know how it would be possible. There was a sense that, for reasons of his own, he was deliberately keeping a certain distance from her until the Boston trip was out of the way.

It was understandable, she told herself, as it would appear to him that she was still emotionally entangled with Simon.

In reality, now that she knew Simon was all right, she found herself letting him go. It was not something that was under conscious control—it was something that was just happening.

What an odd situation she was in, becoming emotionally involved with the man who was helping her make contact with a man she had once loved. No wonder he was holding back from her. No doubt he wanted to witness how she reacted when confronted with her old love. Ironically, she didn't know herself how she would react. Repeatedly, she told herself that she would be strong. In reality, it would be an unknown journey.

'The phone's for you, Anna,' her father called, in the hubbub of activity towards the evening, when the house was milling with people.

'Hi, Anna, it's Seth.' His familiar voice came to her. 'It sounds as though you're having a great time.'

'We are,' she said, a sense of joy suffusing her. 'It's good to hear from you, Seth. My parents have some friends round. Thank you so much for the lovely necklace—I'm wearing it. And Finn loves the building blocks.'

'I'm glad you like it. I'm calling because I've heard from Sophie in South Africa today. They're going to be coming to North America at the end of the second week in January. I thought I would let you know right away so that you can ask for the time off from work. We should give them a few days to settle in before going down there, don't you think?'

'Yes. I…I feel nervous, to say the least,' she admitted. 'Should we meet them at their hotel? Or what?'

'The hotel would be best, I think,' he agreed. 'They'll stay in Boston for at least two weeks as Simon knows people there and he has the medical assessment to undergo, which will take some time. Then they plan to go on to western Canada to investigate the situation with regard to immigration. Simon already has citizenship here.'

'I see,' she said. 'Seth…are you still sure that you want to come with me? I wouldn't hold you to it if you had changed your mind.'

'I'm sure,' he said. 'As soon as you know when you can get time off, I'll book a hotel for us. How many days do you want to be there, Anna?'

'Well, maybe two or three days,' she said, at random.

'Sounds all right. Make it three, then, if we have time on our hands, we can go to a show and do some exploring of the city.'

There was silence between them then, in which she wanted to ask him if they could meet, but the words would not come. Although she sensed that he wanted to, maybe ask her the same thing, he did not do so.

'See you at work, then,' he said finally. 'In a day or two.'

'Yes. Thanks for giving me the news.'

When she disconnected, she felt bereft. She was in no position to take the initiative with him. Instinct told her to leave that to him, if indeed he wanted to do so. From what he had told her about his marriage, it appeared that he was going to be very careful in the future before getting involved again, not to get too involved too soon.

Restlessly, she went into her parents' kitchen and began to clear up the dishes from the running buffet that they'd had over the holiday, serving food and drink to guests who dropped in. Having something to do helped to quell the anxiety of the coming reunion with Simon. So far he was unsuspecting that she would be on the scene. It was possible that he might refuse to see her, if he did not want her to see him as he was now. That was something she would have to deal with if, or when, it arose. If that happened, she would quietly fade out of the scene, leaving a photograph of Finn with Simon's sister. Bit by bit, she was planning her strategy, becoming more realistic as zero hour approached.

Equally, she would have to be similarly realistic with Seth.

Her New Year's resolution would be that she would look to the future, try to put the past into perspective, let go of certain hopes, certain people.

Finn was getting a lot of attention from the people around him, as well as playing with new toys, so she would let him go to bed later than usual. It was a respite for her, giving her time to think.

In about three weeks' time she would be seeing Simon. It hardly seemed possible, that what she had wanted for so long was happening. The reality was often different from one's imaginings. There was an old saying: *Be careful what you wish for because you might get it.* Now she wasn't certain what she wanted. The situation would resolve itself, whatever she wanted as an individual. As soon as she returned to work she would ask the head nurse for a week off in January, while her mother would take care of Finn. If Simon wanted to see Finn, they would have to arrange that for some other time.

Over the next couple of weeks at work the tension built up as Anna tried to prepare herself in every way possible for the meeting with Simon and his sister.

The head nurse had given her the time off that she wanted, with no difficulty; her mother had agreed to care for Finn. As she worked with Seth, he often looked at her speculatively and smiled. 'When this is all over,' he said to her once, 'you'll have a sense of release, whatever the outcome. This has been on your mind for too long.'

She nodded, knowing that what he said was true. First of all she had to get through it. Several times a day she changed her mind about how she would handle the reunion, until at last she got to a point where she decided not to have a plan, to let the circumstances themselves dictate how she would behave.

CHAPTER ELEVEN

ANNA sat next to Seth on the plane to Boston on a cold, snowy day on which the flight was only half an hour delayed because of the weather. For the umpteenth time it seemed remarkable to her that he should be with her, that he had actually arranged to take time out of his hectic life so that he could be with her. They had talked about the fact that Simon was distantly related to him, how that was a motivating factor in his desire for them to meet. Perhaps, Seth had remarked, he could be of some help to Simon in getting re-established in Canada.

The flight was short. In no time, it seemed, they were driving in a taxi thought the snowy streets of Boston, then unloading their luggage at the big hotel, one of a chain, where Simon and his sister were staying. It was one of those comfortable, well-run places where you knew that all your needs would be taken care of automatically, without fuss.

Anna glanced around her as they crossed the very large carpeted lobby, pulling their suitcases on wheels, expecting that she might see Simon. He was not there among the numerous people.

She and Seth had separate rooms on the same floor. As

they went through the check-in process, she asked, 'Can you tell us if some friends of ours have arrived, Dr Simon Ruelle and Sophie, his sister?'

The clerk at the front desk checked his computer. 'Yes, they arrived two days ago. They're on the second floor.'

In the lift, going up to their rooms on the sixth floor, Anna had the feeling that she had little claim on Simon. Reality was very rapidly taking over from fantasy. She let out a sigh, holding herself rigid with tension.

'What are you thinking?' Seth asked, standing close to her, giving her a sense of protectiveness.

'Wondering what I'm doing here,' she said.

'We could get it over with today, if you like. I'll contact Sophie and see what she thinks. If we could meet first, maybe we could have dinner together later on in the hotel dining room. I'm looking forward to meeting Simon and Sophie.'

'A good idea.' Already she had said, several times, to Seth that she was grateful for his presence. Even so, she felt that she would be forever in his debt.

Sometimes it seemed to her that he was testing her. For what? Perhaps to see if she was essentially different from the woman he had married, who had gone for what she wanted in a very single-minded, blatant way, regardless of what he had wanted. Finding a woman who was ordinarily honest, whether he wanted a relationship with her or not, might do something to restore his faith in human nature, in the female part of it at least. So her incoherent thoughts informed her.

Perhaps he wanted to see how she would behave with Simon, what claims she would make on him, if any. Maybe he needed that for his own sense of sanity. Already she was having second thoughts about even being there. All the trouble that she had gone to with Hector Smythe, all the trouble that he had gone to had come down to this—the fear that she had done the wrong thing, that she didn't know how she was going to go through with it.

Thoughts churned back and forth in her mind.

'I'll knock on your door when I've got something arranged,' Seth said, parting from her at her door part way along a corridor. His room was two doors down. 'Have courage.'

Quickly, partly to distract herself, she unpacked her small suitcase, had a shower, changed her clothes in the comfortable, anonymous room, dried her hair with the convenient hairdryer in the bathroom, put on a touch of make-up.

When Seth knocked, she was ready, at least superficially. 'Hi,' he said, coming in and closing the door. 'It's arranged, Anna. I've met Simon.' As he said that, he looked at her soberly, and intuitively she knew that she would find Simon very changed, even though Seth had never met him before. The sick feeling of nervousness deepened.

'I'm as ready as I'll ever be, Seth.'

'I'm to take you down to Simon's room, where you can see him in private. First, I'll introduce you to Sophie. We'll all have dinner together later.'

'I'm so frightened,' she said, picking up her room key from a small table by the door.

'Hey,' Seth said, gripping her upper arms, 'you've come this far and the worst will soon be over.' He kissed her on the forehead. 'You're a brave woman. You can do it. What happens next should be up to him in regard to any relationship he might want with Finn. I'm getting the impression from you, Anna, that any ideas that you might have had about you and Simon have gone. Am I right?'

'Yes…I think so,' she murmured, twisting her door key round and round in her hands. 'I just don't know how I'm going to feel when I see him—that's what I'm frightened of.'

'I'll come in with you, if you would like me to, just to introduce you, even though you know each other. It sometimes helps to have a third person present initially.'

'I'd like that,' she agreed.

There was tenderness between them as they looked at each other. Then he kissed her, gently, on the mouth. 'Come on,' he said. 'We'll go to Sophie's room first, she's next to Simon.'

Simon's sister looked older than Anna had thought she would be. No doubt the long journey from South Africa had tired her as she looked exhausted, even though they had stopped over in France for a few days *en route* in order to rest. The responsibility of being a companion to Simon must also be a great one, Anna speculated as she wondered why his girlfriend, the nurse, was not with them.

'I'm pleased to meet you,' Sophie said, shaking Anna's hand. She was petite and dark-haired, looking a lot like Simon, with a sunburnt face and blue eyes. 'Simon didn't tell me much about you, Anna, but, then, he had brain damage that affected his memory and then his concentration for a long time after the accident.'

'It's really good to meet you,' Anna said, somewhat shyly.

'You won't find him the same person, I'm afraid,' Simon's sister continued, 'so try to prepare yourself for that. He's also suffered from depression for a long time. He does remember you now. I've told him you will be here to see him, but I didn't say you had a child. That will be up to you to divulge, if you think it appropriate after you've seen him.'

'Thank you for all your help,' Anna said, a dark premonition of sadness swamping her. It all seemed rather lame now, what she had wanted for herself, faced as she was with the reality of Simon's tragic life. It wasn't about her any more, it was all about him.

'I have to tell you that there is a woman in South Africa who wants to marry Simon,' Sophie said. 'And he's more or less come round to the idea, even though he won't be able to have any children. I think Seth told you about that?'

'Yes.'

'Her name's Laura and she took the initiative in that. She loves him, whereas I'm not certain what he feels for her—he hasn't divulged that to me. If we come to Canada to live, as we hope to do, they will probably marry before they come. We'll go to western Canada, perhaps to one of the islands.'

'I see,' Anna said, appreciating the other woman's honesty. 'Have you been to see the doctors yet?'

'No. We want to rest for a few days. Then we have several appointments, spread out over a week. Seth will take you next door to see Simon now, then I'll see you both later at dinner. We've reserved a table in the dining room. Perhaps we'll meet for tea as well.'

'Yes,' Anna agreed. The time had come, there were to be no more delays.

Still feeling sick with nervousness as they stood outside in the corridor while Seth knocked on Simon's door, her predominant feeling was one of relief that the years of speculation would soon be over, that she could turn her mind finally to other things after this. Looking for Simon had become an obsession, she could see that very clearly and soberly now. The fact that he was alive was now something that allowed her to let go of the anxiety that had plagued her.

'Come in.'

Anna cast a quick glance at Seth, who took her arm. 'It's going to be all right,' he said quietly.

Simon was sitting in a chair by a window on the other side of a large room and he turned to look at them as they came in. Seth walked with her firmly towards him, his hand lightly on her elbow. There was a wheelchair nearby, reminding her that Simon could not walk.

Anna felt a sense of shock and such a welling up of intense emotion that she felt she might faint. Although the man in front of them was recognisable, just, as the Simon she had known, he was so changed that she felt she might burst into uncontrollable tears. If they had passed in the street she might not have recognised him. He was very thin, and the eyes that he turned on her were dead of emotion, his face impassive. The bones of his face jutted out beneath tight skin.

'This is Anna Grey, Simon,' Seth said, his voice calm and even.

'Hello, Anna. It's so nice to see you.' There was no recognition in his eyes as he looked at her, as he said the polite words, so that she got the impression he hardly knew who she was, that he was going through the motions of politeness because he had been briefed by his sister about who she was and where she came from. 'Come and sit down beside me.' He held out a hand to her, palm upwards, as though he wanted her to hold his hand rather than shake it.

'Hello, Simon,' she said, her voice trembling as she took his hand. This was going to be as difficult as she had thought it would be, and then some. 'How are you? I tried to find you, you know, for a long time.'

Seth brought over a small chair so that she could sit next

to Simon. 'I'll see you later,' he said quietly to her, squeezing her shoulder.

Simon looked at her, holding her hand as though it were a
sort of lifeline and could make him remember. Unable to help
herself, tears welled up in her eyes. He looked a lot older, exhausted, his hands thin and trembling, his face almost gaunt,
even though he was still a young man. Such were some of the
manifestations of the ordeal he had been through. 'I didn't
know what happened to you,' she whispered, 'until very
recently.'

'Don't cry,' he said. 'I'm all right now.'

Anna doubted that he was all right.

'I was incapacitated for a long time,' he said, his voice in-
finitely weary, still giving no obvious indication that he really
recognised her, and he spoke slowly, his words slightly
slurred as though he was on some sort of medication. It was
possible that he was taking antidepressants, Anna speculated.
'When I finally came back to a semblance of reality, the
recent past was more or less dead to me. All I wanted to do
was get back to South Africa where I felt I belonged. My
career was over, so I felt that my life was over. I'm an invalid
now.'

'Oh, Simon,' she said softly. This man was like a stranger,
his sad eyes looking at her as though he did not really know
her. 'Do you remember anything about Gresham? Do you
really remember me?'

'Yes…I do now. For a long time it seemed like a dream,
as though it hadn't really happened. When I came back to
myself, as you might say, I decided I would put that behind
me because I could not go back. I thought of you, Anna, but
then I thought that you were better off without me. It wasn't

as though we had planned to marry or become engaged, it was more or less casual—at least, that was how I remembered our relationship. Something could have come out of it perhaps, given time, but we didn't have the time…did we?'

There was a stab of utter sadness, like a knife in the heart, at his words. No, she wanted to say, it was not casual for me. Instead, she looked at him silently.

'Then it all seemed so distant, especially when I was back in Africa,' he added, listlessly. 'It was all such a mess, and all I could think of was that I would be an invalid for the rest of my life. Now we want to make a new life here.'

As they sat holding hands, Anna acknowledged that this man was not the Simon she had loved. He had grown up and changed, partly because of the accident and perhaps partly because of an inevitable maturation process. The accident has changed him, made him morose and cynical, which was understandable.

'Don't cry, Anna,' he said again. 'I've come to terms with my situation. I can even work, after a fashion, which is more than I dared to hope for just after the accident. And I'm planning to marry.'

'I'm very glad for you.' That sentiment was sincere. Now he belonged to himself—he did not belong to her in any way.

He had said it casually, as though the two of them had not had a love relationship, a passionate affair. It was almost as though it had completely slipped his mind.

'I had brain damage, Anna, which has changed my personality, so that I will never be the same person that you knew.'

All she could do was nod silently.

'I'm very fortunate,' he went on, 'that I don't have to earn a living, even though I do work now, part time. We have family money, which is safe and secure.'

'I have to tell you,' she began, in a rush, wanting to get it over, 'that when you left Gresham, I was pregnant with your baby, Simon.'

'What?' he said, squinting at her as though she were a mirage. 'Pregnant? You were pregnant?'

'Yes, I didn't have time to tell you.'

'Well…that's amazing. I had no idea.' He was staring at her, as though trying very hard to remember that they'd had a sexual relationship. Also, she thought she detected a slight spark of interest in his eyes, together with slight puzzlement.

'I…we…have a son,' she said falteringly. 'His name's Finn—he's a wonderful boy. I thought you ought to know. That's why I've come here.'

For several moments there was silence while he took in what she had said to him. 'I can hardly believe it,' he said, staring at her. 'So you were alone when I should have been there with you. I'm sorry, Anna.'

'You couldn't know,' she whispered, tears gathering again. If she had needed any proof that he was a good man, this was it, worrying about his neglect of her. Seth was a good man, too—that conviction came to her at the same time.

His face was still almost expressionless. 'I can't seem to take it in, because it was the last thing I was expecting. I can never father a child again,' he said flatly, 'unless there's a miracle. And I don't believe in that sort of miracle.'

'Would you like to see a photograph of Finn?'

'I would…yes, please.'

Anna fumbled in her bag for the envelope containing professional photographs of Finn, as well as some very informal small snapshots that she and her parents had taken in the garden at home. 'Here he is,' she said, handing them over into his hands, which shook. 'I…I thought I would give you my address in Gresham, then if you come to Canada and would like to meet your son, we shall be there.'

'Yes…thank you,' Simon said, looking at the pictures. 'Oh, Anna, I should have been with you.'

Pressing her lips together to stop them trembling, Anna said nothing. She had been vindicated, and that would be enough.

'He looks like a sweet boy—and I can see a family resemblance,' Simon said. 'This is incredible… It's going to take a while for this to sink in, Anna. My brain is so tired these days. Of course, I'm delighted. Could I keep one or two of the photographs?'

'Of course,' she said. 'Take as many as you like.'

'Thank you, Anna. Thank you for giving birth to my child, for not giving him up for adoption. He looks healthy and happy.'

'He is,' she whispered.

'You know,' he said, 'sometimes amazingly good things can follow tragedy. I've met Seth, who's related to me, and that has reunited our families again. Otherwise I don't suppose that would have come about. And now you tell me that I have a child when my hopes of fatherhood had been taken away from me. I'm sure you're a great mother, Anna, I can tell.'

'I try to be,' she said softly, wanting to run back to the sanctuary of her room so that she could weep for this young man who had been changed for ever.

Clasping her hands tightly in her lap, she watched him

while he went through the pictures again and again, and chose three for himself. 'I'll show these to Sophie,' he said. 'We're going to meet for dinner, I understand?'

'Yes.' Anna could see that he was tired. 'I'll leave you now, Simon, you must want to rest.' She got up.

'Anna,' he said. 'There's something I want to say to you.' He reached forward and took both her hands, appearing to concentrate very hard on what he was going to say. 'If I'd known…if I'd had any idea that you were pregnant, I would have made contact. I would have done what I could to give you some support.'

'I know you would, Simon.'

'You see…I've been very depressed…suicidal even. It's been a strain on my family. I'm not over it yet…perhaps I never will be. Sometimes it comes over me—swamps me, you might say—and then I can't do anything.'

'I understand,' she said.

'There's something else,' he said. 'Seth is very…taken with you, if that's the right word. I could tell by the way he spoke about you. He seems a good man.'

'He is a good man,' she agreed, a strange relief coming over her, as though Simon were handing her over to Seth.

Just then there was a knock on the door and Sophie came in. 'We're going to have some tea,' she announced, 'in my room. Then a rest before dinner.'

Anna stood there, looking at her. From what Simon had just said, it was as though he had never entertained the idea that they would marry…or if he had done so once, it was so long in the past that he did not remember what such a desire felt like. It was all over and done with, that part of what they had shared. He himself had entered a nightmarish world in which physical and mental survival had been uppermost in his mind. There had been pain and suffering, in which she'd had no part. All she could do for him now was to let him share their son in the future.

'See you a little later, Simon,' she said.

'Perhaps we should go for a walk in the snow, Anna?' Seth said, coming in behind Sophie, as though he were tuning in perfectly to her thoughts and emotions, as though he had been hovering outside. 'You and me.'

'Yes…please,' she said, her voice barely audible.

Simon was very perceptive, she thought, if he knew on such short acquaintance that Seth was 'taken' with her, and she wondered if Sophie had told Simon all about Seth's failed marriage, as he had told her. Because he could not be a partner to her himself, perhaps he wanted to pull in Seth as a father to his son.

'We can have tea first if you like,' Sophie said.

Automatically, Anna moved towards the door, feeling numb with shock and drained.

In the lift going up to the sixth floor, which they had to themselves, Anna responded to Seth's questioning glance. 'I want to cry,' she said. 'It's so tragic. He kept three photographs of Finn. It's not pity that I feel…it's a terrible sense of waste.'

'He's a very brave guy,' Seth said, 'making the best of a bad job. We'll have tea, then put on our warmest clothes and go out for a walk, just the two of us. All right?'

'All right,' she said. 'I'd really like that.'

At tea, Sophie looked at the photographs of Finn. 'He's so adorable,' she said, 'and I can see that he looks like Simon, though more like you, Anna.'

Anna nodded. 'He is adorable,' she agreed. 'He has a very sweet, calm personality.' As she spoke, she found that she could not yet associate this changed Simon, and his sister, with Finn.

Instead, she had the images in her mind of Seth reading a story to her son, carrying him to sleep on a sofa at his house, then carrying him to the car, putting him in his bed later. The realisation was coming to her that she had, without noticing it, come to think of Seth as taking on the father's role with her son, with the added bonus that they were related.

That would not do, because it was not reality. Yet neither could she associate this strange, morose Simon with her sweet Finn.

All the time they were having tea she struggled to control her emotions. Clinical depression was something that she'd had only theoretical experience with, during her nursing training, and had not worked in psychiatry. However, she did not need to be trained to discern that Simon had changed a lot, that he was very low in spirits. Again she wondered if he was on medication, and whether something of his low mood had been caused by brain damage. Later, perhaps, if she got a chance, she would ask Sophie about it.

At the moment she was certainly depressed herself, a sense of sadness like mourning pulling her down. At the same time a kind of strange peace was with her. She was glad that she had found Simon and had imparted the news about his son. Something was finished. Any earlier ideas that she had harboured about perhaps renewing her relationship with Simon, perhaps asking him to help support her son, had disappeared. In the end, everything had become simplified—she had managed to make it clear that she had no demands whatsoever to make on Simon. Even if she had, he was in no position to help anyone, except perhaps financially, and that she would never ask for now.

There was snow on the sidewalks and also falling gently in big flakes as she and Seth walked, bundled up to their eyes in warm clothing. They were both preoccupied with their own brooding thoughts.

Seth took her gloved hand in his as they walked along the streets near the hotel, and she let it rest there. They looked into shop windows to distract themselves from the strong emotions that had surrounded their meetings with Simon.

'I have to thank you, Anna,' Seth said at last, after a silence in which neither of them felt compelled to speak, 'for enabling me to meet my extended family. Without all this I would probably never have made contact with them. And it's amazing that they're hoping to come to Canada.'

'Well, it was inadvertent on my part,' she said. 'I'm really glad that something positive has come out of it for you, Seth.'

'How do you feel now?' he asked.

'Very sad, unbearably so…for Simon, rather than for myself. I forgot about myself, which is as it should be. It was a real effort not to break down.'

'You're right, that's as it should be, I think,' he said. 'It's what happened to him that's at the forefront of my mind.'

'I don't want him to think that I pity him,' she went on. 'I'm relieved now that I know. It's the end of something.'

'There's always a sadness in endings,' he said pensively. 'Even if you know it's the right thing. Even when there's tremendous relief. It's a sadness for lost time, for what might have been, for mistaken judgement…all those things.'

They crossed a street at the traffic lights, surrounded by swirling snow, jostled in the crowds. Seth knew Boston, knew where they were going, so he led her to shops with interesting displays in the windows, to distract her.

'It's not because he's an invalid,' Anna said, renewing the conversation when they were in a quieter stretch of a street. 'It's because what was between us has died. We'll remember it in our son…if Simon wants that. If he doesn't…I won't mind now, because I see that I am on my own in being responsible for my child. For the first time, I don't mind. Finn is with me, and I love him so much, enough for both of us.'

They walked on, feeling the flakes of snow on the exposed skin of their faces, its refreshing coldness welcome, as though it were part of a cleansing rite. Although she did not say that to Seth, Anna had a sense that he was feeling it, too.

'This is one of the strangest days of my life,' she reflected.

'And it's not over,' he teased her, squeezing her hand. 'I've been wanting to say this all day. Please forgive me for casting doubts on your interpretation of events when we first met.'

'It's all right,' she said. 'In your shoes, I expect I would have felt the same.'

'When I get home,' she remarked, 'I'm going to put away that large photograph of Simon that I have on the mantelpiece, to see if Finn will notice. It's the past now.'

'That's probably a good idea. Simon doesn't look like that any more,' he said. 'If Simon comes to Canada, you can possibly get new pictures of him to show Finn, so that Finn will recognise him if Simon decides they should meet.'

They walked for a long time, going round in a large circle, building up an appetite for dinner.

'I'd like to invite you to the hotel bar for a drink before

dinner,' she said. 'I'd like a cocktail, and I'll treat you to whatever you want. It's a small thank you.'

'I accept,' he said.

Dinner was not the ordeal that she had envisaged. They carefully avoided any discussion about Simon's medical condition and talked about Africa instead, and of other places they had travelled to, then of what the family hoped to do when, or if, they came to Canada as immigrants. They hoped to buy land, perhaps a farm, so that they could have an income from that, while Simon hoped to get a limited amount of work as an assistant surgeon in hand surgery, in which he had recently specialised, because that was what he could do sitting down. Already they had real-estate agents looking for suitable land for them.

Again Anna felt her emotions difficult to control when he talked about that, his very limited professional life, even though he seemed grateful that he was able to do something. Before the accident he had anticipated a very promising career as a trauma surgeon, as well as a general surgeon. He had been very skilled at his job.

From time to time she exchanged glances with Seth. He knew precisely what she was thinking.

If Simon could adapt to that, then she could adapt to the life of being a single mother. The troubles that she had to bear seemed paltry compared with his. She was privileged to have Finn.

As they sat at the table, she felt Seth's eyes on her frequently. Through all this he was getting to know her, and vice versa. Yet a lot of the time she had little idea what he might be thinking.

CHAPTER TWELVE

A WEEK later, Anna sat in the sparse office of Hector Smythe for what he called a debriefing.

'Well, Ms Grey,' he said, from the other side of the desk on which he had placed the manila folder, which was somewhat fatter now, 'I think we can say that we have had a successful outcome. Yes?'

'We have,' she agreed. 'I'm very grateful to you, because now I have a peace of mind that I have not had for a long time, even though it's all very sad. I know Simon's alive, that's the main thing, and my original faith in him is intact.'

They had talked extensively about the case, during which she had been able to tell him that Simon had had no idea that she'd been pregnant, that he would have made an effort to support her had he known. From that she had come out with her self-esteem more or less intact, she told him. Simon had not deliberately deserted her.

'I think I can stamp this "case closed".' Hector Smythe smiled at her. Earlier she had handed him the cheque for his services. 'Of course, if you find later that there are any loose ends that need to be tied up, you can come back to me. For instance, if your circumstances change with regard to finances, I can advise you there. It could well be that Simon, of his own accord, will offer to contribute to his son's education and support once he has seen the boy.'

'It's possible,' she agreed.

'I also have some excellent lawyer friends, in family law,' Hector Smythe went on, 'whom I could recommend if you contemplate marriage at any point and your husband wants to adopt Finn but allow visiting rights to Simon Ruelle…if it turns out that he wants them. Of course, you don't have to do any of that if you prefer not to.'

'Thank you. I've decided to wait now to see what Simon will do. I've done all that I'm going to do for now,' she said, looking at him calmly across the desk. 'I feel so much more at ease.'

'I'm glad you've come to that understanding,' he said. 'Um, will you and Dr Seth Ruelle remain friends as well as colleagues?' he enquired politely, looking at her with his very shrewd brown eyes. 'A very nice man.'

'I certainly hope so,' she said carefully, 'but I really can't say at the moment. You see…he has some issues of his own from a previous marriage. And he comes from a very wealthy family—out of my league, you might say.'

'Oh, I don't know,' he said. 'I would make an educated guess that he has more than a passing interest in you, Ms Grey. He told me something about his previous troubles, we were able to discuss them. I wish you both well. I think you would be good for each other, you have a lot in common with your work. And he's related to your son.'

'Yes,' she said.

'Be friends first, that's important,' he said. 'I see a lot of messed-up people in my line of work.' He stood up. 'Make an appointment to see me any time you want, Ms Grey, if need be, for any sort of follow-up.'

'Thank you again,' she said. They shook hands.

After leaving Hector Smythe's office, Anna walked down the street feeling as light as air and grateful to him. The gist of his advice was that one should do the sensible thing in relationships, otherwise impulsive behaviour generally came back to haunt one in a negative way. She felt like laughing aloud with a peculiar kind of joy that came out of relief.

It was a crisp day, with a little snow on the sidewalks and on the trees that bordered them. After years of speculation she felt free and almost girlish again, with a rare sense that life was good. She was young, of course—it was just that most of the time she didn't feel it. As she walked, she swung her bag back and forth, enjoyed the sound of her boots crunching on the snow and the feel of her warm coat as it swished around her legs. The feel of the soft wool scarf around her neck, the hat on her head seemed like new experiences to her that she could enjoy in their simplicity. Tentatively, she could look forward again, perhaps go back to university to take an evening course to get her brain into shape again.

Finn had gone to a play-group for the morning, dropped off by her, to be picked up by her mother. She planned to go to a small bistro for lunch, one that served good French food, where she would also have a glass of white wine. So she would celebrate in a small way her sense of release and vindication. Simon had never been there with her, neither had any colleagues from work—it was her place. One day, perhaps, she would invite Seth there.

In the bistro, sitting near a window where she could look

out at the falling snow, she ordered her food and the glass of wine. From now on she was going to relax and take things a day at a time. A rare contentment made her want to smile, so she opened up a newspaper so that she could have something to focus on and not find herself smiling inanely at nothing in particular.

'Will you come for a quick drink with me after work, Anna?' Seth asked her when there was no one else in the operating room, just after they had finished a case in the afternoon of the next working day. 'I know you like to get home quickly, so we'll make it fast.'

He pulled off his operating cap, ran a hand through his thick hair and wrenched the disposable face mask from around his neck. In the two-piece green scrub suit he looked very masculine and powerful, his broad chest and shoulders reminiscent of a soccer player's. As always, Anna had trouble not staring at him. Some of the other nurses had no such qualms and ogled him openly.

'I'd like to come,' she said. Since the Boston trip she had been tense with expectation and also a fear that Seth and she were destined to revert to a working relationship only. Unaccountably, she suddenly felt shy, lacking in confidence, as she wondered how he had judged her, how he had seen her over this fraught period.

'Meet you in the main lobby, then,' he said, 'as soon as possible after work, then I'll drive you home if no one else demands my presence here. We won't go to the pub over the road. I know another place that won't be full of hospital personnel, another unpretentious little pub.'

Anna smiled and nodded, then began to clear up the room

which was in a mess after the case. They still had one more, relatively straightforward case to do.

Happiness suffused her as she stripped the operating table of its soiled cotton cover and began to swab it down with a disinfectant solution, going about the very familiar tasks efficiently and automatically, while her mind jumped ahead to the meeting with Seth. Such happiness was something that she had not felt for a long time, and she had wondered whether she would ever find it again with a man. At the same time she cautioned herself to be careful, not to read too much into Seth's interest in her until she knew more about him.

'Do you want to scrub for this, Em?' she asked her colleague when Emma came back into the room. 'Or shall I?'

'I'll scrub, if you like,' Emma said. 'You've done more than your fair share of scrubbing today, and over the past weeks.'

'OK. I'll be the circulating nurse for this one, then, although I don't mind scrubbing. I really like it.'

Soon they were ready, Emma had scrubbed and Anna wheeled in the patient on the stretcher. All was going efficiently and well, one of those well-oiled days, and it actually looked as though they would be getting off duty on time.

'This young woman,' Seth said to Anna and Emma when their patient was under the anaesthetic, 'is having a lobe removed from a cirrhotic liver. It's a sad case, because she got hepatitis C from a blood transfusion. She's been trying to become pregnant for years, but has spontaneous abortions, which may have something to do with the state of her general health. Maybe after this she'll be luckier.' As he spoke, he looked directly at Anna, holding her gaze for a few seconds, so that she could tell he wanted her to know he thought she was fortunate to have Finn, not to think of him as a handicap in any way.

She smiled at him, letting him know that she hadn't done so, and never would. The young woman, small and frail, clearly unwell, could have been her in different circumstances. Yes, she herself was blessed.

Seth met her in the main lobby as arranged. In fact, he was there a moment or two before she came.

Dressed in her warm winter clothes, her full-skirted coat coming well down over her high leather boots, she looked charming, elegant, beautiful and innocent, he thought as she walked towards him. Her soft fair hair fell almost to her shoulders, framing her pale face and making her look deceptively fragile. Now that they no longer had what he thought of as the 'Simon question' hanging between them, perhaps they could move on from here.

He was aware that he had been a little stand-offish at times, blowing hot and cold. Although he had found it in himself to be kind to her, from a genuine desire to help, had told her that he wanted a 'you and me', he knew that he had held himself back somewhat, making the assumption that if he did not do so he could get involved in a way he was unprepared for. Since the trip to Boston he could see that such an attitude was perhaps presumptuous and that Anna would not take any sort of initiative with him. Yes, he had been somewhat arrogant there. They smiled at each other.

'Just a minute,' she said, 'while I put on my hat and scarf.'

Through the large revolving glass doors to the outside they could see swirling snow being blown by the wind. 'Looks cold,' Anna said, as she wound a scarf several times round her neck, planted a woollen hat firmly on her head and put on gloves. 'Ready!'

They drove in his car to a pub a few streets away. There was a wood fire burning in the cosy bar, so they found a small table near it.

'I'm just going to have Irish coffee,' Anna said, 'with just a little bit of brandy.'

'Good choice on a day like this,' he said, taking off his coat. 'I'll have the same as I have to battle the elements with the car.' He went to the bar to place their order.

Anna stared into the fire, not wanting to remove her outdoor clothing until she had warmed up.

Back beside her, Seth started to speak. 'I asked you for a drink, Anna, because there's someone I want you to meet, who…' he looked at his watch '…should be arriving any time now.'

'Who?' she said.

'Wait and see.'

A moment or two later a tall young woman, dressed in a very smart black coat—which did not look quite warm enough for the Gresham winter—and an expensive-looking black fur hat came into the bar and looked around her.

'Excuse me.' To Anna's amazement, Seth stood up and walked towards the young woman who, she could see, was very attractive. A strange, sick feeling of apprehension came over her. Was this why he had asked her if they could be friends? Because there was never going to be anything else?

As they both walked towards her, weaving through the tables in the pub, she knew that the blood was draining from her face. Anxiety replaced her former mood of tentative happiness.

At the table, the young woman removed her fur hat and ran a hand through her thick, glossy hair, which was the colour of polished mahogany, and looked at Anna assessingly. Her eyes were dark, almost black, and her skin was a pale creamy colour.

'Anna, this is Laura Ashcroft. She's Simon Ruelle's fiancée,' Seth said.

'Oh!' Anna struggled rather clumsily to her feet and held out her hand. 'How do you do?' she said. Relief, greater than anything she had ever experienced, flooded over her.

The other woman took her hand and said hello but did not smile. Instead, her large expressive eyes searched Anna's face. There was even a certain hostility about her, Anna thought as she returned the gaze.

Seth pulled out a chair for Laura, and they all sat down.

'Laura's passing through Gresham on her way to Vancouver to link up with Sophie and Simon,' he said. 'They've extended their trip and are there looking at property.'

Seth kept his features more or less expressionless, although Anna could tell that he commiserated with her in her surprise.

'Why didn't you tell me before?' Anna said to him.

'I thought it was better this way,' he said.

'That's very mysterious.'

'Would you like a drink?' Seth asked Laura, who was peeling off her elegant black suede gloves.

'I'd love a whisky and soda, please,' she said.

When Seth went to the bar, the two women looked at each other. 'I wanted to meet you, Anna, so I approached Seth, whose name I got from Sophie. You see, I didn't know about you until Sophie told me, and I didn't know that Simon had a child. I thought I should talk to you about what is going to happen in the future. You see, I love Simon very much. I hope that one day his disability can be improved on.'

'Well, I can understand that,' Anna said, somewhat nervously. 'I'm very pleased to meet you. Please, don't think that I will interfere with your life in any way—'

'But you will,' the other woman broke in passionately, 'because you are the mother of Simon's child. You will have to interact in some way.'

'That will be up to Simon,' Anna said. 'And you also, to a certain extent.'

Seth came back with the drink.

'I want to know what this is going to do to my relationship with Simon,' Laura went on, visibly upset. 'I...I don't think you thought of me at all.'

What she'd said was true, Anna had to acknowledge with a certain feeling of shame, realising then that she had sort of assumed that a young woman who would marry Simon would take him for better or worse. What did that say about her, Anna?

'I...don't love Simon,' Anna said, thinking aloud, 'and he doesn't love me. We respect and like each other, I think.'

'I suppose you pity him?'

'No...I don't think so. I feel empathy for his situation—it's tragic. I didn't know about you at first when I started to look for Simon. How could I?'

'I'm trying to consider that, but if you think I'm jealous—yes, I am,' Laura said, after taking a gulp of her drink. 'Jealous of the child—and of you.'

'Please...you don't have to be,' Anna said, beginning to

feel desperate. 'Believe me, I understand your situation
and how you feel. It will be up to Simon whether he sees
Finn at all.'

'Why don't I have to be jealous?' the other woman persisted, her voice shaking, and her hand also as she lifted the
glass to her lips. 'I feel that I'm in a very peculiar situation
now. I could have a baby, but Simon wouldn't be the father.'

'May I say something?' Seth, asked, looking first at Anna,
then at Laura.

Anna nodded. 'Yes. I didn't anticipate this, I must
admit…and I'm sorry for that.'

'Laura,' Seth said soothingly, 'there is one very good
reason why you do not have to worry about the resurgence
of a relationship between Anna and Simon. Anna and I are
more or less engaged…we love each other. We've kept it
quiet up to now because we wanted to get this issue with
Simon and Finn sorted out. Now we have got it sorted out.'

'I… We…' Anna said, expelling a breath as her jaw
dropped in surprise. Trying to cover up, she sipped her coffee.

'Is that true?' Laura challenged, looking from one to the
other. 'You didn't even hint at that earlier, Dr Ruelle.'

'It's something very private between the two of us,' Seth
said smoothly.

'Anna?' Laura Ashcroft said to Anna.

'Um…it is true…of course,' she said.

'When are you getting married?'

'Oh…' she said, struggling for words, 'not as soon as you,
but…'

'Not long after,' Seth finished for her.

The hypocrite! Anna thought. Wait until I get him alone!
Coming out with all this glib stuff, then probably taking it as

sort of a joke as soon as Laura is off the scene. He fancied himself as a sort of peacemaker. Anger and frustration were building up in her. What was he playing at?

'And what about the little boy?' Ms Ashcroft said.

'We haven't finally decided on that,' Seth said. 'It's probable that I would adopt him, as I am related by blood. He could take my name or keep the name he has now, his mother's name, of course. That will be up to him when he understands what it's all about.'

The liar! Anna thought, staring at him, trying not to look stupefied.

'And Simon's visiting rights?' Ms Ashcroft said.

'That will be up to Simon,' Seth said. 'And, of course, Finn as well. When Anna and I are married, he will no doubt come to see me as his dad. I'm hoping so, anyway.'

Hell! Anna thought. How can he be so smooth? This woman would find out eventually that it wasn't true.

'Can I drive you back to your hotel?' Seth asked Laura as she finished her drink. 'I hope you have a good vacation in Vancouver, which won't be as cold as here. We'll all meet again when you're living there and settled, I wish you the best, you and Simon.'

'Thank you,' the woman said, standing up. 'I'd appreciate a ride.'

'I'll just pay the bill.'

Seth got to his feet, meeting the frustrated glance of veiled fury that Anna shot him before going over to the bar. She stood up as well, studiously gathering her hat, scarf and gloves.

'Congratulations,' Laura said. 'Seth didn't even hint to me that he was planning to marry you.'

That makes two of us, Anna thought furiously. He was setting her up and then would let her down with a crash, and would no doubt be amused.

'I guess he knew that I wanted to meet you anyway.'

'Yes, he's a great mind-reader when he wants to be,' Anna said tartly.

'He's such a nice man, a truly lovely man.'

'He can be.' Just wait till she got...

'And he's a Ruelle, too. Such a strange coincidence, that he is related to your little boy. They're such a grand family. I feel privileged to be part of it.'

'Really?'

'They were like royalty once, you know, in their part of the world,' Ms Ashcroft said, a touch of awe in her voice.

'I didn't know,' Anna said, trying to keep sarcasm out of her voice. And I'm not sure I want to know now, she thought. Perhaps I could have made an educated guess, she thought—that's why I thought he was not for me, latterly, either Simon or Seth.

'There aren't any royalty here...although some have pretensions,' she added. 'They are generally insufferable.'

Fervently she hoped that Ms Ashcroft loved Simon as much as she professed to.

'You'll find out. Such an amazing family,' Laura said.

'"How are the mighty fallen"' Anna quoted.

'I wouldn't say that. Just changed.'

'Ready, sweetheart?' Seth said to her, coming to stand by her side, taking her arm. 'I'll drive Laura to the hotel first. Then we'll go home.'

'Home?'

'To my place.'

Laura gave her an interested look that managed to convey the sentiment, How sweet!

'I…' Anna said. He was ushering her forward, then out the door into a blast of icy air and falling snow. His suggestion implied that they were having a sexual relationship, or so she thought, her anger mounting. Laura clearly thought so.

'I do love this snow,' Laura said, smiling at them, again seeming to think how charming they were as a couple.

They drove Laura to her hotel, where Seth got out of the car to see her in the door. When he came back, got in and slammed the car door, Anna was ready for him. 'What the hell are you playing at?' she said.

'I'll explain when we get to my place,' he said, starting the engine.

'I don't want to go to your place,' she protested, near tears. 'I'm late as it is. I don't like playing games. You should have let me deal with that woman. And why didn't you tell me about her beforehand?'

'She was very upset. She was crying when she phoned me, so I though of this way out. Apparently Simon looks at the photographs of Finn a lot and has one of them by his bed…so Sophie informed Laura. She fears that Simon doesn't love her as much as she loves him.'

'Maybe she's right. How do I know? I can't help any of that,' she said. 'Simon is Finn's father after all. I'm planning to have a DNA test done on Finn to send to him.'

'Good,' Seth said, somewhat curtly.

'It's true that I didn't think very much of her,' Anna said, her voice breaking with emotion. 'I should have done—I can see that now—and I'm ashamed.'

'Good,' he said again.

They drove through the snowy night, as fast as weather conditions would allow. 'I want to go home,' she said, her voice shaking. 'All those lies you told…that was unforgivable. I thought you didn't tell lies! You were so self-righteous before…'

'We have to talk,' he said. 'I'm fed up with this Simon issue. It's about time it came to an end.'

CHAPTER THIRTEEN

AT HIS house, he parked in the driveway right by the front door. With no choice, Anna followed him into the house and stood in the hallway while he put on lights and patted the dog.

'Let me take your coat,' he said.

'No. You tell me first what you're playing at,' she demanded. 'I'm very upset and angry.' She took a swing at his face, wanting to slap him, but he caught her hand. 'How can you say that we're getting married—that we're getting married soon?' She imitated his voice derisively. 'And all that stuff about adopting Finn. How dare you?'

He was still holding her arm. 'How dare I what?'

'Play with my emotions like that! Putting on an act.'

'It's not entirely an act. I'm somewhat fed up with the role I've been in since we got back from Boston, and before that, to a certain extent.'

'It was largely of your choosing,' she said, raising her voice.

'Why are you so upset?'

'I'm upset because for me it's not an act.' Her voice broke and tears filled her eyes. 'I really do love you. God help me, I tried not to.'

'I know you do, Anna,' he said wearily, dropping her arm. 'You're like an open book.'

'Then why…?

'Because I've had enough, I guess, of waiting for you to come to me. I want you, and I don't know where I am with you. This was an opportunity to come out with it.'

'You want to make love to me? So that's it! It's payment time, is it? You think that because I have a child that I'm easy?'

'No! Very definitely not! I don't think that.'

'I want to go home.' Anna turned away from him to lean against a wall, hiding her face, sobbing.

Silently Seth came up behind her and put his hands on her shoulders. Then he put his head against the back of hers, so that his mouth was near her ear. 'I love you,' he said softly. 'I love you, Anna Grey. Like you, I tried not to, but I do. I love you and I trust you. So, you see, I don't just want to make love to you…but that, too. There's been too much suppressed emotion between us, mainly because of Simon getting in the way. Now I want it to be about you and me, Anna. Me and you.'

She said nothing, but continued to cry softly. He kissed her ear.

'I don't believe you,' she mumbled.

'It's true. I think I fell in love with you when you first came into my office with what seemed an unlikely scenario.'

'I'm fed up with not being trusted by you.'

'I just said I trusted you.'

'And I was humiliated in front of that woman, with that story you came out with,' she rushed on. 'I didn't know what to say, or how to act.'

'I wasn't lying,' he said. 'It was all true, all what I want.'

'Laura said you Ruelles were like royalty. Well, I'm not a princess.'

'What? That's rubbish.'

'I don't think it is.'

'If you say no to me, I'll let you walk home,' he teased.

'You would, too,' she said, glaring at him, slumping back against the wall. 'My mother is expecting me home. She must be wondering where I am.'

'I'll call her and say you're having supper with me.'

'Exercising your charm?'

'Mmm.'

'What if I don't want to be here with you?'

'I would respect that,' he said, drawing her into his arms, nuzzling her ear. 'I think you do want me. Take your coat off. You must be hot with the central heating blasting away.'

Anna let out a sigh, tremulous with longing for him, which she was trying not to let him notice. 'So I'm an open book,' she said. 'It's a pity you weren't a little more open.'

'I've bared my soul now—in front of a third party, too,' he said. 'You could say I've burned my boats. I'm at your mercy.'

'Oh, shut up,' she said. 'I don't believe you.'

'And I wish you would be a little more original.'

'This is not an original situation,' she said. 'Smooth, glib, attractive man trying to get woman into bed. I'm at a disadvantage—you're eight years older than I am, and much more experienced. Simon is the only partner I've had.'

He laughed, and she felt, in spite of herself, her own lips forming a smile.

'I have a habit of becoming pregnant,' she said.

'I wouldn't call once a habit,' he said. 'I'll make sure you don't—not that I would mind.' He lifted her face up and smoothed the hair away from her temples. 'I would like it, in fact. I love you and I want to marry you.'

'How can I believe you? You're such a...such a dark stranger.'

'I'm trying not to be. Tell me again that you love me. Look at me while you're saying it.'

Disarmed, at least partially, Anna did as he asked. 'I love you,' she whispered, lifting her face up to his and staring him right in the eyes.

'Say it again.'

She did.

'Now say, "I will marry you, Seth." Or you can call me darling, if you wish.'

'I'm not going to say that because I still don't believe you.'

'Why not?'

'Because, as you said, you're messed up. So am I.'

'I love you,' he said. 'Whether you stay with me will be up to you. If you do, afterwards you can agree to marry me...or not, as the case may be.'

'You mean...sort of trying you out?' she said.

'If you want to put it that way,' he said, laughing. 'It's more that afterwards you'll know I love you.'

'Oh...' she said, expelling a breath on a sigh.

'We'll have a glass of chilled white wine, if you would like to, so that we can calm down, then I'll drive you home if you don't want to stay with me now. In a day or two I want to take you out to dinner and go down on bended knee to ask you to marry me. In the meantime, you can think about it. I think we've been friends for a long time...long enough.'

He unbuttoned her coat so that she could shrug out of it, then he sat her on a chair and pulled off her boots, much as she pulled off Finn's snow boots, taking his time about it. That gesture alone melted her, but she wasn't going to let him see it…not yet.

She sat on a sofa in the sitting room while he went to get the wine, which he uncorked in front of her, then took two long-stemmed glasses from a cupboard.

In turmoil she watched him while he poured and handed her a full glass. With his glass, he touched hers. 'I think I should propose a toast,' he said. 'To us, love, and to our future together. To Finn and to our other children.'

'Don't take too much for granted,' she said, giving him a sidelong glance that she tried to make furious.

Inside she was bubbling over with a tentative happiness that was threatening not to be tentative for very long. And she was beginning to be curious about what his bedroom looked like, as the rest of his house was in such superb taste—even if it had been created by an interior designer.

They sipped the wine. 'This is very good,' she said, nervous, wanting him so much but frightened to admit it. Simon was no longer between them. Now it really was just the two of them. If this was what she wanted, if he was the man she wanted, she had to have the courage to take him.

'It's from the Ruelle vineyards,' he said. 'It's your turn now, Anna.'

Shyly, she touched his glass with hers so that it made a delicate tinkling sound, forced to follow his example. 'To our love. To you, Seth, for all you have done for me and for coming into my life. To a dark stranger who from now on I hope will never be a stranger again.'

'Not angry with me any more?'

'Only a bit,' she said. 'I've made up my mind.'

'What?'

'I want to be with you, now and always,' she said, quietly, seriously. 'Will you always be with me?'

'Yes. I promise to love you and cherish you for the rest of my life. As I said, you have my trust as well as my love.' With that, he lifted one of her hands and placed a kiss on the palm, folded her fingers over it. 'Hold my promise tight and remember it always.'

'I will,' she said.

They drank a toast to their future, and Seth took her hand. When their glasses were empty, Anna stood up and put out both of her hands to him.

4 FREE

BOOKS AND A SURPRISE GIFT!

We would like to take this opportunity to thank you for reading this Mills & Boon® book by offering you the chance to take FOUR more specially selected titles from the Medical™ series absolutely FREE! We're also making this offer to introduce you to the benefits of the Mills & Boon® Reader Service™—

- ★ **FREE home delivery**
- ★ **FREE gifts and competitions**
- ★ **FREE monthly Newsletter**
- ★ **Exclusive Reader Service offers**
- ★ **Books available before they're in the shops**

Accepting these FREE books and gift places you under no obligation to buy, you may cancel at any time, even after receiving your free shipment. Simply complete your details below and return the entire page to the address below. You don't even need a stamp!

YES! Please send me 4 free Medical books and a surprise gift. I understand that unless you hear from me, I will receive 6 superb new titles every month for just £2.89 each, postage and packing free. I am under no obligation to purchase any books and may cancel my subscription at any time. The free books and gift will be mine to keep in any case.

M7ZED

Ms/Mrs/Miss/Mr ....Initials ....

BLOCK CAPITALS PLEASE

Surname ....

Address ....

....

....Postcode................................

Send this whole page to:
UK: FREEPOST CN81, Croydon, CR9 3WZ